A NEW KIND OF BIO-WARFEAR

Kane spun back around in time to see Mariner raising his unwhole hand from the broom handle to cup the air over his head like a guerrilla readying to toss a grenade or a wizard readying to lob a spell.

"Say hello," Mariner snarled, "to my little fucking friend, cocksucker!"

Mariner's hand swept forward through the air, and Kane wondered if the guy did have some kind of antipersonnel explosive device. When his hand finished the stroke, it was a perfect pitch. Almost Red Sox material. However, it was not a ball that he lobbed. Not an explosive pineapple or mystic ball of napalm, either. It was his finger.

The dead man's ring finger the little shopkeep wore in place of his own missing digit — the not quite rotten token of vanity — broke off and launched through the air like a tiny spear. It was no longer curled. Now, it was as arrowlike straight as a finger could be.

The surreality caught Kane off guard, but the worst was the way the thing twitched on its approach, curling in a fraction, baring the ragged nail like the shield and spearhead in a phalanx line.

The best training for martial arts became as secondary as instincts. Kane ducked without consciously deciding to, and the finger passed overhead. From the scream, it hit one of the skagheads behind him. A glance revealed new depths to the horror:

The dead flesh curled and straightened, curled and straightened, crawling up the spearman's flapping cheek like an inchworm, homing in on the man's eye and then gouging deeply into the soft orb . . .

Wormtown

Walkers

By:

Daniel R. Robichaud

(writing as C. C. Blake)

Twice Told Tales

Houston, Texas

USA

2015

Parts of this novel originally appeared as the novella *Kane and the Hungry Dead* by C. C. Blake. Vampires 2 Publishing. ©2012.

Valkyrie Force 1: Wormtown Walkers is ©2015 by Daniel R. Robichaud
Excerpt from *Valkyrie Force 2: Damnation Driven* is ©2015 by Daniel R. Robichaud
Cover Art © solarseven
Cover Design © 2015 by Twice Told Tales

Published by Twice Told Tales
All rights reserved.

If you have any questions, please contact the publisher at daniel.robichaud@gmail.com.

Dedication

For Trista, Mamalade and Sappho,
Three gals worth fighting for.

Storm Front Advancing

The Mayor could see no sign of storm clouds through the leaded glass windows in his third floor office of Wormtown's fortress-like City Hall, but the thunder was nevertheless evident. He tapped a thoughtful fingertip against his chin, other hand occupied with holding the elbow near his midsection; he did not have a gut, per se, he was much too thin for such fleshy luxuries. He frowned at his own scattershot thoughts.

Wormtown. Worcester's nickname was a disgrace, even in these already disgraced times. A name that reminded one of festering nonsense. The city was anything but another corpse, like Boston to the east or Amherst to the west or Hartford to the south or Providence to the south by southeast . . . Those places had gone dark years ago.

The survivors had come here, and now they were outside these windows. Three floors down and hard at work. All the men, women and children who had flocked to the promise of safety and who possessed skills he wanted or services the skilled needed. One thing the end of the old world had done was reset the clock. Sure, as the old world had crept toward its climax, people carried smartphones instead of .44 revolvers and hybrid smartcars tootled around the city's narrow streets instead of horse drawn buggies and carriages, but the doom-filled day the dead returned had taken a hammer to the cultural clock, resetting the calendar to somewhere around the time of Wild Bill Hickok and the expanding western frontier. Of course, these days the frontier expanded in all directions at once.

The door banged open, and panic once more intruded on the Mayor's calm sanctum. "Sire, there's been another disappearance." This news came from Slown, the Mayor's second, a toadish fellow with large yellow eyes and a larger pale belly, a fellow who was squished into a Seersucker suit because he thought they connoted station, when all it did was make his bulging eyes look even more provocative and his body decidedly sausage-like.

The Mayor glanced back to his second and continued tapping the thoughtful finger against his chin. "How many does that make?" He knew the answer already, but keeping a toad feeling helpful was one way to control that toad. Have him respond in expected fashion, and there would be no nasty surprises.

"Five, sir. Five of our, well, not quite best and brightest, but five shining lights."

"We cannot tolerate a single loss," the Mayor snapped. "Scientists are in short supply these days. We don't exactly have universities churning them out anymore, do we?"

He recalled the days of his own graduation, receiving a piece of paper and then being told there were not enough jobs for the numbers of PhDs that were being pushed out of the system, all the systems around the country. Long gone, those days. Now, the brains that earned those papers in those supersaturated years were once again too few to waste.

A funny coincidence, since those brains made them appetizing to the undead threat roaming the world.

"And who is it this time?"

"Another biochemist," Slown said. "Trini something or other. Married to that physicist who operates out of the old clock tower."

"I know the one." The Mayor recalled her as a classy redhead with brown eyes and an impressive rack. She had been smart enough, sure, but even better: she could communicate. With Phase One of his plan nearing completion and the need to move to Phase Two, he would need proper communicators. Bother. "What leads do the Protectors have?"

His police force was more the latter part of that equation than the former. Force was easier to muster, but actual policing was a difficult task.

"Clues are yet to be deciphered. We suspect Fowler, though."

The Mayor spun on his toady with an uncharacteristic snarl. "Of course it's Fowler. Everything is Fowler, these days. It stinks of that Mad Doctor. Why are we surprised he's involved? Answer: we're not. For as long as this city has been rebuilding, he has been demanding we pay him fealty. And every time we have refused, he has pulled some stunt to pull us into line with the rest of his fold." The Mayor caught his tongue, then. Chuckled softly to release the rage. "Next, you'll be telling me more rumors of armies amassing. Or secret government laboratories under our very feet."

"Those," the toady said, "are the rumors, yes."

"And they are also nonsense," the Mayor said. "Don't you think we'd have found out otherwise by now? Our Protection Services do have an Intelligence division, and at least two of the agents is worthy of the name."

The toady looked confused. Possibly on the verge of tears.

Valkyrie Force

"Besides, aren't the walking dead enough of a menace?" the Mayor muttered. "Do we really need to worry about our own species trying to bone us for a percentage?" He sighed, and rapped his knuckles against the wood of his desk. "I want answers. That fellow, the ambitious Protector."

"Kane," the toady supplied.

"Yes, that's the one." Again, the actual name was a known quantity, but allowing Slown to fill in the blank brought him once more under control. *Make them useful or make them dead*, it was the only way to play politics in this ostensible-Democracy-actual-dictatorship. "You think he can produce results?"

"He's got ideas," Slown said, as though such a thing were verboten in his world view. "But he seems clever enough. Smart, even."

The Mayor did not have the heart to tell his toady that he had used synonyms instead of denoting separate qualities. "Let's give him a modest budget, let him run. At best, he solves this issue. At the very worst, he hangs himself."

"You're a wise man, Mayor."

"Thank you, Slown." Using a man's name created the illusion of friendship almost as much as sharing intoxicants or sports facts. "You're a good man, too."

"Sire?"

"Yes?"

"What if there is something to them?"

"To what, pray?"

"The rumors? Armies. Laboratories. Those things? We haven't proven they don't exist."

The Mayor's chest heaved with a sigh, as he debated the merits of explaining why disproving hypotheses was the more important concept than proving null hypotheses. "Why, then we will have to deal with them, won't we? And Kane strikes me as a solutions man." Quite a bit of the Force in that one, with an equal measure of the Policing as well.

"As you say, sire."

After his toady departed, the Mayor returned to his window and waited for the next peal of thunder to resound. It might come from the horizon, from far off. He suspected it would originate far closer, however. Perhaps even rise from the outermost ring of pacified Wormtown's residences. Perhaps over on Boylston street over near the dusty halls of Worcester Polytechnic Institute not five miles away. Or it could be in the park outside these very windows where local landmark statuary stood, one representing the local-born soldiers lost in war and the other celebrating youthful vigor (the infamous Turtle Boy).

Even now, dissidents skulked down there, despite Protection Services' best efforts to keep the rabble from settling in any one place.

Thunder sources. Dozens of them. Hundreds.

He tapped his lip, wondering at how best to lance the boils. And whether or not cauterizing them afterward would prevent future growth.

Chapter One

The Cum Dumpster's claustrophobic confines grew all the more sinister from the pall of smoke hanging over the bodies of deep dreamers and scag addicts. Though the windows still sported posters for the latest XXX DVDs and the sign out front announced this as an Adult Superstore, the place had stopped being a jerk-off's paradise shortly after the old world ended in blood, fire and the walking dead. It had become a new sort of dick cheese dumping ground since then.

Upon entering the place, Kane found himself holding his breath, as though he might catch airborne despair like a disease. He scanned the crowd, trying to discern corpses from the comatose. All the collapsed still seemed to be breathing.

Unlike the other addicts and rejects in residence at the Cum Dumpster, Mariner did not sprawl upon the floor. Instead, he moved in careful, practiced steps amongst those bodies, sweeping the litter away from them, playing good little store minder. The Cum Dumpster, if it could be said to belong to anyone, belonged to Mariner and that made him the best source of intelligence this side of the fattest walking dead's swollen stomach. Why Kane came to him first of all.

Upon seeing his former compatriot, Mariner waved a dismissive hand and muttered, "We're closed. No more room. Go find somewhere else to waste your precious time, Protector."

Standing six feet three inches tall and weighing two hundred twenty pounds of solid muscle, Kane towered over the five-foot six-inch Mariner. However, the good little shopkeeper showed neither fear nor signs of backing down. This was no surprise for Kane. In the ugly world built atop the bones of one that peaked just before the dead began to walk, the subservient did not last long on their own.

The Cum Dumpster's tender was not an old man, in truth. He had been kicking along this round world for maybe twenty-five, twenty seven, surely no more than thirty years. However, his proclivity for chemical perversion had given him that poorly preserved quality most often found in the bed ridden oldsters abandoned to uncaring retirement communities where every room was a coffin and every meal was served via tube or drip by an apathetic staff.

Mariner wore a gray suit coat as though what once communicated Wall Street power and success still offered some armor in this world. Kane preferred his own uniform's Kevlar vest and the black plastic bite guards on his ankles and forearms. Still, Kane could not argue with Mariner's show of spine. There were no apparent armaments aside from the chipped and dented handle on his big headed shop sweeper. Wasn't that welcoming?

Kane's weapons waited within easy reach: a semi-automatic pistol remained in the black leather break open holster on his right hip, while his combat knife remained in its sheath tied to the left. The big man showed his palms in a gesture he hoped to be non-threatening, though he knew quite well that his hands alone were large enough to crush paint cans. "I didn't come here to fight, man."

A pair of desert dried bones rubbed together: Mariner's laughter. "Then take your partner and get lost."

Kane frowned. If anyone would have an insider's knowledge to the mystery of the missing scientists, it was this man. Keeping him happy might prove the best way to get the information; however, keeping him breathing until he talked was the real primary objective. "Partner? I'm alone, friend."

In fact, Kane had not come alone. Dougie Majorca was outside the decrepit pleasure house in the jeep, keeping an eye on the street.

Mariner's scowl deepened. "I believe that like I believe the dead will all permanently lie down tomorrow. I believe that like I believe Silvia Saint will then show up offering a free round of BJs for any and all interested parties."

"Look," Kane said, "I have a question and you can answer it. I can maybe make it worth your while."

Mariner's scowl broke, however, and he bared his thirteen remaining teeth in a gold-yearner's grin. "You got some cans, maybe? Or a broad out there? I haven't had sight or sample of beer nor clam in a wicked long time."

Kane considered the case of canned goods in his trunk, including a six pack of brown beer bottles all full and freshly capped that his team had salvaged from a roving raider group's holy cooler; that six pack had sat in near reverential glorification even if the beer had turned to piss. He said, "Former, yes. Latter, no. I don't sell skin."

"You could maybe make a go of it," Mariner said. He twisted the broom handle round and round between his hands. "You look like a fucking barbarian. Speak true: your biceps have triceps, don't they?"

Kane cocked his head. "We talking or not?"

"You ask if we're talking? Negotiations is already happening, Kane. Didn't you notice?" He turned the broom handle in short, sharp circles through the air between them. "Words is passing back and forth between us, ain't they?"

"Nothing of value, though."

"So you say. I'm clocking you in ways you'd never expect."

It was then that Kane realized some of the scagheads were in different orientations. Mariner could trash talk pretty well. Distraction was a talent, and Kane had to admit the good little shopkeep possessed it in spades. The big man had been concentrating on the not-talk enough to miss the knives being readied and the nail studded clubs being unwrapped from their beggar's rags until it was almost too late.

Kane sighed, "This going to get messy?"

Mariner's grin turned into a full on leer. "You got cans, you say. But I'm betting you don't have anything to pay me back for before. Remember the *last* time I did you a solid?"

Of course, Kane remembered. There had been a little difference of opinion about drugs coming into the newly fortified city. Mariner had been a bagman in those days, earning cans and ration-chits with a smile, a whispered word, and a courier's bag stuffed with cocaine. That difference of opinion had ended with a sudden surgical operation performed by sixteen crazed men with machetes and chainsaws. When things had gotten crazy, a pack of six starvation maddened undead had broken out of cages and made an already crazed scene even more of a madhouse. Both Kane and Mariner had gotten away from the internecine with their lives. Mariner's banishment from Whoville had come soon after.

Mariner continued, "It cost me plenty then and you never once made amends. You got an extra ring finger in there I could maybe sew on?"

Kane glanced down to see the good little shopkeep's left hand clutching the broom handle. "Looks like you beat me to it, Mariner."

Poking through dirty boxer's wraps, a not quite rotten black man's ring finger curled around the broom handle almost like it belonged there. Almost, except Mariner was of Italian heritage and not African.

"Did I?" Mariner puffed his chest irritably, like a lizard preparing to spit venom. He glanced at the finger and laughed. The first promise of relaxing tensions. "So I did. Not many have noticed my little piece of vanity." He locked eyes on Kane's, again. "I always underestimate your deductive reasoning, Sherlock. It must be your size, yes? We believe large equals clod."

Kane did not drop his guard. "All right, Mariner, enough is enough. You want me to bow my head and acknowledge that you're the man? I want to work this out." He bowed his head but never broke eye contact. If a man held eye contact with a dog, it was a challenge; if a man broke eye contact with a hyena, it was surrender.

"You came here for business, is that what you're saying?" Mariner countered. "Well, you're outside the king's limits. This is the borderland, Mr. Kane, between the last bastion of life and the tyranny of the dead." After a pregnant pause, he smirked and added, "When you die out here, no one notices, no one cares, and no one avenges."

Skagheads stood in the shadows, filling and emptying their chests as though the art of breathing required concentration. The way they held their makeshift weapons was natural enough. Here was a crew more accustomed to dealing death than coping with life.

"You going to kill me?" Kane asked. His hands dropped to his waist. "I'm here with a peace offering, man."

Valkyrie Force

"But not an apology," Mariner snapped. "You come in here swinging your dick like everyone want a suck, but I'll be damned if you actually say what I need to hear from you? That mess was your fault. That brain-eating cocksucker chowed down on *my* hand because *you shoved my ass in the way*. And I'm supposed to be grateful you bring me scraps?"

Kane released a breath. The dickering period was well past done. He wondered if this mob would let him walk out the door, or make their move now.

Mariner did not snarl for his cronies to bring him Kane's head. He did nothing melodramatic or even overt. Just dropped his gaze to stare pointedly toward the floor, his chin bobbed twice as though he was enduring a minor epileptic twitch, and then all hell erupted in that small space. The shadows boiled forth with a dozen active bodies.

The skagheads surged forward with weapons raised, snarling. Ready to give their master a few pounds of flesh in return for another hit.

If Kane had had time to consider their plight, he might have felt for this sorry lot. However, he did not have time to spare. This world was made for cannibals, and a survivor had to chew and swallow when the situation demanded.

The first skaghead to come into killing distance was a dark complexioned man flipping a pair of nunchaku through the air. The weapon whirred like a helicopter propeller, rusty nail studs promising plenty of pain. As the weapon whipped forward to lay first claim on his blood, Kane shot his boot into the wielder's groin. Steel toe collided with skaghead testicles hard enough to rupture. The junkie's face twisted in a mix of surprise and agony. His nunchaku clattered to the floor, and he glared at Kane through tears.

A pasty white kid in his late teens, neck and arms marked with enough tracks to make him look like a smallpox survivor, appeared behind the nunchaku swinger. He had two butcher knives and the sort of face even a mother might wince away from. Prison tats clouded his cheeks with blue-green abstractions, magic symbols of some kind.

Kane caught the nunchaku wielder by his ears. Dragged him off his feet and threw him sidelong into the knife-swinging maniac coming alongside his right. One butcher's knife buried in the meat of the human battering ram's upper arm. The two skagheads went down hard.

Kane's ears alerted him to additional footfalls coming from behind. He snatched his knife from its sheath and spun on his heel, going into a low crouch for protection. Three fair complexioned men with dirt encrusted dark hair were coming. One carried a spear like it was no different than a sword, all value of reach the weapon might offer lost in the skag cloud. The other two carried baseball bats overhead like they only had only ever used axes.

The Emerson CQC-7B was one hell of a knife. Kane lashed out, opening the spearman's left cheek; a slab of meat fell from occipital bone to chin and blood sprayed all across the baseball bat man's face on that side. Spearman recoiled, clawing at his face. The first bat dude turned hurriedly aside, momentarily blinded, and slammed into the remnants of an old DVD rack.

The third man got his lick in, however. A double fisted slam sent his slugger into Kane's right shoulder. The big man's arm went instantly numb. His knife clattered to the floor.

Kane drove his left palm up, aiming for the bat dude's nose – worst case scenario: break the nose and blind the man with water; best case scenario: break the cartilage and send the splinters into the man's brain – and missed completely. The skaghead was fast on his feet, wild eyed and grinning like a damned fool.

Kane carried through, using the attack's momentum to drive his entire body forward, shoulder blocking the bat dude. He was too close for the bat to do anything terrible. Kane's shoulder drove into the man's chin, and his knee drove into the man's gut. The slugger went left and its wielder flew backward, caught the old front counter with the middle of his back, and folded the wrong way with a hearty crunch of shattering vertebrae.

Kane spun back around in time to see Mariner raising his unwhole hand from the broom handle to cup the air over his head like a guerrilla readying to toss a grenade or a wizard readying to lob a spell.

"Say hello," Mariner snarled, "to my little fucking friend, cocksucker!"

Mariner's hand swept forward through the air, and Kane wondered if the guy did have some kind of antipersonnel explosive device. When his hand finished the stroke, it was a perfect pitch. Almost Red Sox material. However, it was not a ball that he lobbed. Not an explosive pineapple or mystic ball of napalm, either. It was his finger.

That black man's ring finger the little shopkeep wore in place of his missing digit – the not quite rotten token of vanity – broke off and launched into the air like a tiny spear. It was no longer curled. Now, it was as arrowlike straight as a finger could be.

The surreality caught Kane off guard, but the worst was the way the thing twitched on its approach, curling in a fraction, baring the ragged nail like the shield and spearhead in a phalanx line.

The best training for martial arts became as secondary as instincts. Kane ducked without consciously deciding to, and the finger passed overhead. From the scream, it hit one of the skagheads behind him. A glance revealed new depths to the horror:

The dead flesh curled and straightened, curled and straightened, crawling up the spearman's flapping cheek like an inchworm, homing in on the man's eye and then gouging deeply into the soft orb. The skaghead spearman let out a shriek of agony, trying to swat the finger off. He only managed to drive it deep into the socket. Then, it was gone, rooting around the insides on a beeline for brainpan before too long.

Kane whirled back around to face Mariner. The crazy bastard had a living dead finger he used like a weapon! What other tricks might he have up his sleeve?

Kane rushed the tin pot dictator of this porn castle, and Mariner's face went from gloat to cringe in seconds. Then, the remaining mob pig-piled on the big man, driving him to the floor. As the sea of bodies carried him down, Kane saw a new level of gloat swell Mariner's cheeks and bug out his eyes.

"You're a stupid motherfucker, coming in here alone," Mariner said. "Boy, you so should have brought broads." Mariner waved a live index finger in a circle around his head. In military jargon, that signal meant a team needed to huddle up ASAFP, but for the good little shopkeeper it was a clear indicator of the glossy posters and stand ups featuring old porn queens and glistening body parts. "I see this skin all day, every day but it's as fake as a nun's smile. Real skin, man, it's the one thing I can't never have. Well, no skin except for that leper bitch back in Peep Show corner, I guess." He glanced off to the left, toward one of the gray-cowled skaghead bodies still lying near a little doorway with faded messages painted overhead:

FULL NUDE PEEPS!

50 cents per 1 minute.

WHAT A DEAL!

Valkyrie Force

Mariner wiped his lips like a drunk eager for another sip. "And I ain't so proud I can't admit I've been wondering if having my meat rotting off might not be a price worth paying for a little bit of slick fuckery. I'd a told you all about the Hangsaman Boys if you brought me a fuggly life support system for an even a halfway decent pair of titties and a mostly clean clam." Now, he faced his men again. "Cut that cocksucker's throat, shoot his partner outside, and someone get me my finger back."

A sudden thunderclap announced a shotgun's report. Mariner's chest exploded. He dropped to his knees staring at the red rain on the floor that had once been bits and pieces that had been locked safely inside him. He reached down, fumbled with a pair of chunks as though he might be able to reassemble them and then he collapsed into a twitching heap.

As soon as their lord and master dropped, the mob on Kane scattered. Half fled for the doors, a quarter of them stared at Mariner's corpse, and the remaining two guys rushed the source of the blast – it had come from that peep booth. A shroud swaddled woman, the leper Mariner had mentioned, was up on her knees, a short barreled shotgun in her hands. She worked the weapon's pump action with practiced ease, racking a fresh round into the chamber and blasted one of the attackers off his feet. The other was going to nail her, Kane knew, before she could rack another round.

He dragged his pistol out of its break open holster and popped off two rounds. In general, the Desert Eagle was a massive weapon and heavy as hell. The barrel and clip on Kane's sidearm had been swapped out to enable the use of .50 caliber AE rounds, which were hard to find but worth the effort. His shots were award-winning tight midway between the man's shoulder blades, not that this mattered too damned much. The man's back might show two little holes, but his front would be a royal mess. Even cut down for handgun sized, a .50 caliber shell did enough tissue damage before exiting to fit a man's fist. The target jitterbugged a couple more steps before the woman blasted him off his feet only a tenth of a second later.

Wow, she's good. She had cocked a new round into her weapon's chamber, sighted and fired in half the time it would have taken the most well-trained Protection Servicemen.

Kane pushed himself upright, gun coming around on the remaining skagheads. They showed their palms in surrender, a few crashing to their knees like regular attendees at Protector shakedowns.

Outside, an automatic weapon opened up. Kane's partner Majorca mowing down fleeing skagheads.

The big man had little hope of a positive outcome from this lot, but nevertheless he asked, "Any of you bastards know anything about these Hangmen Boys?"

"That's 'Hangsaman Boys'." This from the leper with the shotgun. She added the period to her response by racking a fresh round into the weapon.

Kane cast a sidelong glance her way. Though her face was covered with bloody bandages, Kane suspected she might well be smiling. "Thanks for the assist," he called. "What do you know about them?"

"It wasn't an assist," she said. "I saved your ass."

Her voice was stronger than he imagined a leper to have. *It makes her sound almost normal*, he thought and then chastised himself for stereotyping.

He had to admit she was right, though he did not verbalize this confession. "Be that as it may," he said. "You know the group?"

"Hangsaman Boys are a raider gang," she said. "They got a clubhouse in Auburn where they keep their rigs and sharpen their blades. Sometimes they make their way into the city. Mariner here greased a few

Wormtown border guard palms. Or do you prefer Whoville, Sergeant Kane?"

Not just his name, which she might have picked up from his conversation with Mariner. She seemed to know his rank in the Protectors, too. His preferences for the city's name for god's sake. Her voice was ringing no bells for him, and the rags did a fantastic job of hiding her identity. "Do I know you, miss?"

"Probably not," she said. "But we know you. What are you going to do with those three?" She indicated the fellows who had surrendered. "Killing them is your style, right?"

"Tales of my bloodshed have been greatly exaggerated," he said. "At least unarmed prisoners."

She shot the one in the middle. The fellow who had first dropped to his knees. His guts spilled, his life ended. A cheap, small caliber pistol clattered to the floor from the dead man's sleeve, stopping its spinning dance when the slide tapped against Kane's boot.

"Now," the woman said, "they are unarmed men."

"Right. You lot can chew floor," Kane said. "Until we are gone. Roger?"

The two remaining men laid face down, keeping their hands visible and their submission clear.

Then the front doors burst open. A man in combat armor and helmet appeared, carrying an MP-5 submachine gun. The barrel still smoked from recent use. Dougie Majorca was an athletic man, five foot ten and lean but by no means wiry. His Native American heritage was evident in the hawkish nose, slender brown eyes, and the Silver Tomahawk proudly pinned to his chest. He scanned the area, and targeted on the woman, saying "Armed tango, boss!"

"Stand down, Majorca. She's on our side." Kane glanced back at the woman, who was unwinding the bandages from her face. He almost glanced aside when they fell free because who wanted to see the ragged mess hiding beneath? But then, he realized she was not a leper at all. She was a lovely woman with striking eyes – one a muddled blue, the other a vibrant green.

"I'm call sign Valkyrie," she said. "Protection Services Intelligence division."

"Valkyrie, huh?" Kane nodded. Hell of a call sign alright. Perfect for a warrior woman. "Well, thank you for saving my life, Valkyrie. What can you tell me about these raiders?"

"That depends," she said. "What are you buying me for dinner, tough guy?"

Despite himself, Kane smiled at the woman's refreshing, up front quality. If she really was Protector Intel, then she was a tough cookie. The smile she flashed him showed she possessed pure brass balls.

"You got any allergies I should know about?" he asked.

"Nothing food related," she said. "Did I hear you say you had cans? What say we pop three open and pool our resources?"

Kane thought that sounded just fine.

Chapter Two

Majorca had gunned down three Cum Dumpster escapees. The bullet-scrambled remains lay in twisted heaps, cracked eggs left to fry beneath the noontime sun. The others were long gone.

Majorca guided them back to the jeep, slipping behind the wheel. Kane slipped into the passenger seat.

Valkyrie smirked when she asked, "Isn't this spot secure enough for you, Kane?"

"Not quite," he said. "It's been pacified for the moment, but scavengers are sure to come along before too long."

She pulled herself up into the jeep's rear and sat down atop one of the two extra-large coolers holding the precious cans and bottles. There, she hooked an arm around the roll bar and loaded fresh slugs into her weapon. Here was someone accustomed to getting things done on transport, Kane noted.

Majorca asked, "So, where from here, Top?"

Valkyrie Force

Kane considered this question for a moment before saying, "Let's inspect the outer wall for holes." Behind him, Valkyrie chuckled. Every soldier knew it was not a matter of holes, but of how big the holes were.

"Affirmative," Majorca replied, and the Jeep's engine roared to life and carried them south.

When the men who would later be crowned Mayor and Council had organized Worcester into the fortress city it now was, they had done so in steps. First, they fortified a central hub; second, they identified an outer ring that could be walled in safely and speedily; third, they performed systematic search and destroy operations on each of the buildings between the safe core and that wall. The living dead did not use any tactics more advanced than "lumber toward the enemy, try to tear them apart and/or eat them." It was a living brain that adapted; the walking dead were hungry as hell, but they were about as adaptable as Commodore 64 computers.

Once the interior was cleared, it was time to split forces into sustaining and exploratory, one to patch and perfect the erected wall and the next to move on to another ring. After long enough, a decent sized space was pacified, and the sustaining efforts dwindled in favor of other efforts -- urban farming and other life sustaining efforts. The walls with the most reinforcement were carefully guarded, but the outermost were left alone for the indefinite future. Between safety and extremity lay a no-man's land perfect for little ne'er-do-well joints that catered to select antisocial clientele.

The outer wall around this section of Whoville – Kane refused to call Worcester by that odious other nickname Wormtown – was notorious for its failures, and it sat not quite three blocks away from the Cum Dumpster. Any fools who sauntered out of the fortified wall through the well-guarded Checkpoint Nuance and subsequently made their way south to Dead Hooker Pond or Clark University beyond it was taking their lives firmly in hand. The Cum Dumpster squatted midway between that manmade puddle and the once prestigious university.

The stretch of wall three blocks down from the Cum Dumpster was made of welded blue steel Dumpsters, shopping carts reconfigured with a blowtorch, chunks of asphalt, and hastily mortared bricks salvaged from a blown to hell shop, which might once have housed a Dunkin Donuts. It looked about as sturdy as a snowman during April thaw.

The jeep pulled to a halt about ten yards from it, and then Majorca turned the thing in a tight U, pointing their ass end at the wall. From beyond the barrier came soft moans. Maybe the walking dead or some victims the skagheads had jacked and left to turn. It was a bad way to go, left behind for dead.

"Alright, call sign Valkyrie," Kane said, turning in his seat to eyeball the woman for the first time since the Cum Dumpster. "Why don't you tell me . . ."

Words failed him.

The woman had shucked her rags, revealing a pretty and curvy specimen of womanity. *Check that*, Kane thought. *This is a dynamite woman*. Call sign Valkyrie was a peaches and cream blonde beauty with a scatter of freckles across her nose and cheeks. Her attractiveness was a bold one, unbroken even by a not quite faded trio of scars below her right eye. Powerfully built, not skinny like an old world beauty queen. She was a warrior woman, capable and determined, and she radiated pure appeal – sexual, intellectual, physical.

"Why don't I tell you what?" she asked. "Cat got your . . . tongue?"

He shook his head, trying to clear it of the lusty thoughts filling it, and then he smiled at the woman. "Tell me about these Hangmen Guys."

"First of all," she said, "they are called the Hangsaman Boys. Second of all, I mentioned they're raiders. They have an interest in flesh, women and child slavers."

"Pedos?" Majorca asked.

"Not directly," she said, "but they've been known to set their boats into the pederast port during fleshless storms."

"Classy," Kane said. In a world as uncertain as one where the dead outnumbered the living and yearned for their flesh, children were an invaluable resource. According to the Mayor, it was every man and woman's responsibility to feed the Whoville gene pool by siring at least three before they were forty. Kane had not even scratched his quota yet, but he figured he still had time. He wanted to find the right set of breeding hips. Check that, he really wanted to find an honest to Christ partner to do the deed with. In Whoville, the odds were good, but more often than not the goods were odd. "And they squeak through the checkpoints?"

"They know who to bribe," Valkyrie said, "or they know how to avoid checkpoints altogether. There are hundreds of hidden ways into our fair city, places the walking dead can't go and most folks won't try."

"And this clubhouse," Kane asked. "You know where it is?"

"Not so fast, hotshot. This isn't an 'I'll jack my jaw until I'm dry' deal. This is a tit for tat relationship. Spill your guts. What took you over to Mariner?"

Kane and Majorca exchanged knowing glances. Majorca was a cards to the chest sort. Kane, however, knew that playing the give-and-get game was worthwhile with a trustworthy sort of player. Though he had no way of knowing for certain, Kane liked this Valkyrie chick for more than her rack and the shape of her face.

He said, "We're on the trail of some missing scientists. A biochemist just vanished. She's number five to go. A lot of the city's brainpower is going who knows where, and though some ugly rumors are circulating—"

"Fowler, huh?"

Kane considered this woman with all the answers. Was she maybe a spy for the mad doctor of the wasteland? She did not seem that way, but he supposed Mata Hari had been a pretty good conversationalist, too. He said, "We are interested in truth, not speculation. Mostly, we want those people back in one piece."

"I hadn't heard about scientists," she said. "Mariner was not into specifics unless he was in his personal zone of silence." Before Kane could ask for clarification, Valkyrie said, "It was a soundproofed back room where he took his big shooters. Even I could not infiltrate or bug that room, at least not in the limited amount of time that I had before you came stomping in. However, I did get that he was in cahoots with the Hangsaman Boys."

"Which I got, too."

"I picked up more. The Hangsaman Boys are in league with a big time buyer. Someone with guns, drugs and cans galore. 'Bling and bang-bangs out the ass' was the technical term I heard. Maybe Fowler?"

"Maybes don't—"

"I know, Kane. You want facts. I deal in facts, too. But any worthwhile fact-finding venture starts out as a fishing trip. You toss the line into the water of rumor, and wait for something to take your bait."

"What bait did you use?" Majorca asked.

"A girl never reveals her secrets."

Down the block, a couple of freaks in gas masks stalked into the Cum Dumpster. Did they have harpoon guns? Kane shook his head in disbelief. The old Massachusettsians were a sea faring race, what with all the whaling museums and such, but these guys were over an hour inland for that sort of thing. And while an hour might not be too impressive in a place like Texas, in Massachusetts it was just enough time to see half the state.

"Think we should head out, Top?"

"I think the girl has earned her beer," Kane said, "and someplace safe to drink it. Take us through Nuance, and maybe over to Shrewsbury Street."

"Affirmative," Majorca said.

As the engine rumbled to life, Valkyrie socked Kane in the shoulder. The blow was brief but surprisingly solid. He rubbed his arm, grunting, "What the hell was that for?"

"I am not a girl," she said. "I'm all woman."

"So you are," Kane observed. She cocked her head when he gave her a brief but visible appraisal.

"You do that again," she said, "and you'll lose one of your eyes."

"Sorry," he said. The apology came straight from the heart.

Valkyrie, however, did not seem to buy it. "Sure you are, buddy. Sure you are. Just remember, if you want me to stick around for a little longer, then you had better afford me the respect I deserve."

"Are you sticking around?" Kane asked, surprised and suddenly hopeful.

"For a while," she said. "You wrecked my information sources here. I might as well see what info I can gather before you destroy every avenue I might want to explore."

"Ooooh, burn," Majorca whispered.

"What was that?" Kane asked, and Majorca said nothing.

They were passing the Cum Dumpster when a horn sounded from the burned out building across the street, a former Laundromat from the appearances. Before the jeep could travel five more feet, one of the gas masked freaks burst out of the porn shop's bullet riddled front doors, gloved fingers and tunic slick with gore, a newly claimed scalp sloshing side-to-side on his belt, harpoon gun held like a chin up bar over his head, screaming like a banshee.

It was a *stay away from my kill* dance, territorial pissing for a post-apocalyptic world. It was a cowardly thing to do, human hyenas claiming someone else's kill as their own.

Kane cast a wary eye to either side of the street, slipping his pistol out with a slow hand to prevent a mob assault. Even hyenas could be dangerous when banded together. Majorca hit the pedal a little more, gunning the engine to get them out of the danger zone faster. Then, a shotgun blast blew the dancing savage off his feet, and from behind both men, Valkyrie roared, "My kill, you bastards! Mine! You leave them where they lay!"

After they had turned a corner, without additional incident, Majorca said, "You know they're going to strip those kills. If you wanted souvenirs you should have collected your ears before we left."

"Ew," said Valkyrie.

"Those hyenas might have turned on us," Kane said. No judgment in the statement, simple curiosity.

"Never," she said. "If we had rolled by without glaring them down, the freaks would have been all over us. You never look away from a hyena. You meet their eyes and stare them down or else you become prey."

Kane considered this, and then laughed. Majorca chuckled too, but in a curious *don't antagonize the crazy person* way. "You're a hell of a warrior," Kane admired.

Valkyrie Force

"Don't you forget it," the woman said. "Let's skip Shrewsbury Street, though. Find a nice quiet hole on the other side of Checkpoint Nuance. Lording over jackals, hyenas, and mutants is thirsty-making business."

"You heard the lady, Majorca."

"Affirmative."

Chapter Three

Valkyrie put away two bottles with little more than a grimace at the first taste of the brew's flat, lousy flavor. No complaints after that. Kane admired a soldier who could *head down, ass up and shut the fuck up* through the less than pleasant patches life had to offer. He had been in one too many hot zones with one too many complainers both in the old world and this walking dead new one, had seen the way they had gotten others (and eventually themselves) killed with their whining.

This woman is something special.

When he came to this realization, he pushed it down. This was neither the time nor the place for heart cord plucking, harps and connection thoughts. *KIP-Kay*, he thought. The mock-ronym had been a keepsake from his first commanding officer. *Keep it professional, Kane.*

Majorca had no such compunctions. After the first beer, he asked, "So what do you like to do when you aren't infiltrating rat nests and staring down kill-thieves?"

Valkyrie Force

"I love long walks across battlefields at sunset, just when the vultures are descending," she said, "and of course karaoke. What girl doesn't love karaoke?"

"I've known a few," Majorca said, and the two of them laughed.

Kane allowed himself a smile.

"One of those two things I said was for real, and the other was a total lie. I'll give you a hint: I don't like hanging out after beaked carrion eaters come to feed. No matter how pretty the sky might look. What about you, hunkahunka?" Valkyrie turned her attention Kane's way. "Are you a full on warrior-poet or maybe a warrior-painter?"

"I don't have a lot of time for that kind of thing."

Valkyrie laughed so hard, it almost sounded like a snort. "Time? You can't be on call 24-7. Nobody can do that without cracking. So, what is it? Painting or poetry?"

"All right, I don't have the patience for—"

"Patience? That's a code for 'my dick is too hard to be gay,' isn't it? The Celts and the samurai were nobody's bitches, and they had non-death-dealing hobbies. What are yours?"

Majorca said, "I haven't ever heard you talk about what you do during R and R, Top."

"We're doing it," Kane said, raising his bottle. "But apart from this? I do have one idle pursuit. I don't get nearly enough time to play around with it."

"You have a girl?" Valkyrie asked the question on both her and Majorca's minds.

Kane shook his head. "Carpentry. I like making things with my hands. Working a lathe, a jigsaw. Staining wood. You know. It can eat up as much time as you dedicate to it, though."

"Holy shit," Valkyrie said, "Kane here is a regular Jesus."

"Far from it." This time, despite himself, Kane joined in with the laughter.

Valkyrie's strong gaze shifted away from Kane as she asked, "And how about you, Majorca?"

"Me?"

"Yes you," Valkyrie pointed the bottle at him, real as a gun. "The slob drinking the beer across the table. The driver with a hardon for MP-5 submachine guns. What's your hobby?"

"I used to make beer, back before the world ended. Nowadays, that's out. There's nowhere to get the hops, the yeast, and everything else. The batch that's just about ready for bottling is the last one I'll make."

Valkyrie jolted as though struck. "You make beer? Honest to goodness fresh beer? Then, why are we drinking this old swill?"

"Because I don't keep it," he said. "Making it is the hobby. Once that's done, I trade it for foodstuffs that my kids can eat. I don't get paid enough to feed all five of them. They deserve better than Whoville's standard brat-rats, at least I think so."

Kane knew the rations for children (the so called brat-rats) were supposed to be mineral fortified and oh so good for growing bodies, but were about as tasty and chewy as boiled shoe leather.

"What kind do you make?" Valkyrie asked.

"I've saved the best for last," Majorca said, "I've got a stout as my going out of business brew."

"No shit?" Valkyrie asked.

Kane said, "I'll pay you for a couple bottles."

Majorca considered this solemnly, then a grin spread across his face. "Deal. Once we get through this, we'll dicker over prices."

Chapter Four

The Hangsaman Boys clubhouse was cunningly disguised as an old dive bar just off the Turnpike. As another brilliant dusk gave way to twilight gloom, Kane twisted the focus on Valkyrie's binoculars to refine the view, but he smirked at mankind's reliance on meaningless symbols and tradition. Even from their observation point atop a six floor Best Western half a mile away, the three infiltrators could tell this locale was exactly the sort of place that one would expect an outfit calling themselves the Hangsaman Boys to ... well ... *hang*.

It was the sort of one story brick and wood joint the big man recalled from the bad old days. Judging by the L-shape and the size, it looked large enough to house a drinking space served by a fair sized bar, a tiny dance floor where strutting motor jockeys could show off their biker mamas, maybe an office spot and storage room in the back, maybe a small live performance stage too where garage bands could show off their half assed covers of Steppenwolf, and of course the bathrooms. Places like these, Kane recalled, had a similar decoration style for the Men's that consisted of cutouts from old sex mags, be they bike stroke books or actual skin rags. All or some of these spaces might have been converted to other uses. In this case, a couple of men walked sentry duty along the rooftop, armed with rifles or crossbows. The parking lot was dominated by wasteland rides, hogs kitted out with armored plating and spare fuel tanks or gas chugging SUVs refitted with ethanol burners and weapon mounts. A sign flanked by two arc sodium lamps declared the place to be *Rider Heaven* in fifteen foot tall, flame wreathed letters. A smaller set of letters assembled beneath warned all comers *This is Outlaw Country*.

"Windows are blacked out," Kane said. "Probably fortified on the inside. Judging by the rides, we could be dealing with as many as twenty people in there."

"Glad we've got a shotgun on our side," Majorca said. "I'm picking up rf signals coming out of there. Can't isolate the channel, so they must have some kind of scrambling tech."

"That means someone skilled enough to use radios *and* scramblers?" Valkyrie asked. "These aren't just another group of hyenas. They're a national club."

"National clubs still exist?" Majorca asked. Kane had been wondering the same thing.

How could banditos and scavengers manage to accomplish what the cities themselves could not? The big towns he had heard about – Worcester, The Pitt, DeeCee, San Diego, San Antone, and Frisco -- acted like fortress cities of old, self-governing and in a state of constant rivalry with the others. For cities, long distances murdered coexistence. Bike gangs should be no better . . .

"Sure," Valkyrie said, fitting fresh cartridges into the magazine of a well maintained Dragunov sniper rifle. "It all comes down to leaders with that magical trio of vision, drive, and the guts to kill infidels and the insolent. In the case of the Hangsaman Boys, they have a National Chief called Cutter Wise. Cutter has a handpicked council, seventeen loyal boys and gals to rule the individual chapters. He keeps *them* in line by some method I can't divine, possibly implanted poison or explosives. Zealots, however, are pretty reliable. And his council of seventeen seem to be pretty zealous to the gang's cause."

"Anarchy?" Majorca asked. "Is that their cause."

"Try: Profit," Valkyrie replied. "Through a couple of channels. But anyway, the council decapitates anyone stupid enough to stick his neck out too far on the rebellion road. Rebel against the cities or anyone against the gang? That's fine for them. Rebel against Cutter Wise's plans? You get your head mounted on a ride as warning. Look at the biggest land yacht down there, and you'll see a catalog of folks too stupid to know their places and shut their faces."

Kane trained his binoculars on the largest of the vehicles, a Ford Expedition with a crude looking machine gunner's turret added to the cargo bay rear. No less than seven heads, in varying states of decay from maybe a week old to a single sun-bleached skull, decorated that ride's front end.

"Well," Majorca said, "that's one way to get ahead."

"Puns, now?" Kane dragged the binoculars away from his eyes and cast a disappointed glance toward Majorca. "I should shoot you on general principle."

"I love a good punster," Valkyrie replied, patting the smaller man's arm. Majorca fairly preened at the contact, and something in Kane's gut twisted.

Focus, he told himself. *The mission is top priority. Figuring out these feelings can wait.*

"Our objectives," Kane said, "are not to bring a national club down, but to locate the missing scientists. Who do you believe would have that information? If we can nab a few minutes of their time, then we don't need to assault superior numbers."

"Nab a few minutes?" Valkyrie asked. "You sure have a pretty way of saying kidnap. I use 'Acquire an asset', myself"

Kane chuckled. "Well, I suppose that shoe fits just as snuggly on the foot in question."

"What I wouldn't give for a mortar," Majorca said. "Just point it over there and start lobbing shells down on the parking lot. Take out their movers pretty well."

"And maybe take our target," Kane said. "Speaking of which, you have any intel on him?"

"Her, actually," Valkyrie said. "The Hangsaman Boys' head honcho here was born without benefit of a penis, and she seems to be doing pretty well regardless."

"Her then," Kane acknowledged. "This leg breaker have a name?"

"Catherine Wheels," Valkyrie said.

Majorca snorted. "For serious?"

"Heart attack serious," Valkyrie said. "She's a hammer thrower, all right. Blond and built like my call sign."

"What about a chainmail bikini?"

Valkyrie cocked a curious eyebrow at Majorca. "Who said I own one of those?"

"I meant Wheelz, aw jeez." Majorca looked away, but not fast enough to hide the blush.

"If you turn any redder," Kane said through a broad smile, "you might pop like a blood blister."

"So, what's the plan for taking Catherine Wheels in?" Valkyrie switched tracks so fast that Kane was convinced her brain was a supercomputer. "She won't come quietly, and will try to take as many of us down as she can."

"Providing it's fair fight," Kane said.

"We fight dirty," Majorca said, "when we have to."

Valkyrie nodded, knowingly. "It's the only way for good to triumph over evil. So, what's the plan?"

Kane dropped the binoculars to his chest and considered the options. Three versus large numbers said a frontal assault was the worst idea. However, if they could convince the leader to come outside to a place of their choosing, they could pull a 'Leonidas and his 300' trick. A well-fortified position could be defended by a handful of people, even three. He could not think of anything nearby, however. Nor could he think of a way to get the woman to come out, short of offering her something she needed.

"No plan as yet," he said. He drew the binoculars back up to his face. "For now, we observe. Unless you happen to know a way to make them scramble out of their little home."

"Actually, I might have an idea." This came from Majorca, not Valkyrie. He was looking west, not toward Rider Heaven, but along the interstate. Kane glanced that way, saw a walking caravan on the move along the interstate's edge.

Valkyrie grimaced. She raised her rifle to her shoulder, and studied the caravan with the weapon's telescopic sight. "Hungry dead incoming."

"Don't fire," Kane said. He felt a damned fool after the words were out of his mouth. It got even worse when he received the scolding.

"Thank you for crediting me with a modicum of sense," Valkyrie said, and then added an icy, "Oh, wait." She paused a moment, moving her rifle while she rattled off numbers and distances. She ended up with twenty seven tangos about two hundred yards out.

Valkyrie Force

"I'm listening, Majorca," Kane said.

Majorca smiled and told them.

After listening to the plan, Valkyrie declared, "That's some pure grade-A bugfuck crazy." To Kane, she added, "I love the way this guy thinks."

Kane chuckled, but the response was a bit forced. The attention she was giving Majorca was driving him to distraction. "It could work," he observed. "But it's an unnecessary risk, splitting our forces like that."

"Don't worry about me," Valkyrie said. "I'll have the best seat in the house, and enough e-rats to keep me running strong. Bar the door and I'm good to sit for a week or so."

"Spoken like a true American sniper," Kane said. "Are you alright running the dead zone part of the operation, Majorca?"

"Roger that," the small man said. "I suggested it, so I'll take the funnest part." His smile was unrestrained, a full on excrement-gobbler's grin.

Kane let out a sigh. "All right," he said. "Let's get this operation up and running before I come to my senses."

"All right!" Majorca said.

This would be better with more people, he thought. However, the modest budget the city had granted him was not enough to deliver actual bodies into Kane's service. Several barracks of Protection Services personnel were sitting on their duffs available, but with the little freedom The Mayor had told Slown to give them, they were in a pickle. The procedure had to be run in the Lifecycle method: first came information gathering. Once that was done, they could acquire bodies for a limited amount of time. The number of bodies and the amount of equipment they would be given was based on the assessed threat level immediately resulting from the information they gathered. Report too soon, and those resources would be wasted – a mouth-breather like Slown would not see the need to waste valuable people in rousting an outlaw biker bar beyond the safe limits. Not unless there was a guarantee of valuable intelligence to be gained. Or a solution.

As much as Kane hated the fact, he had to play this scenario out with just the three of them. Still, that was one more person than he had originally had to work with.

~*~

Kane made his way on foot toward Rider Heaven, remaining wary of hidden sentries and, worse, hidden caches of the hungry dead. He moved slowly and steadily, Valkyrie's voice guiding him through his earpiece. He found a place to hole up sighting distance from the bar, but not close enough that he could just saunter up to the front door and knock.

Kane squatted in a gas station operator's booth, surrounded by bulletproof glass, a ransacked cash register, and a few packs of lite cigarettes. The latter were those sorts of cancer sticks that no one wanted to smoke anymore. Long life was not an option for most, so if a person was going to pollute the lungs then it might as well be with the good stuff. Preferably unfiltered.

He left the binoculars hanging around his neck, as any reflection of light off the lenses would be a dead giveaway to his position. He groaned at his own accidental pun. Dead giveaway, indeed . . .

From his belly bag, Kane produced an old protein bar. Despite the age, it was still chewy, almost moist. In some cases, preservatives were a soldier's best friend. With three bites, the thing vanished into his cheeks and between his mashing teeth on a short trip to the gullet.

Waiting was the hardest part of any covert gig, and this little scam was going to be truly surprising if it worked without a hitch. Really, it was an easy way to find some facts. How the Hangsaman Boys responded to a troop of marching dead walking past their front door would be insight they could not have wished for otherwise. And if, for some unforeseen reason, Kane found himself with the opportunity to acquire their target, then it would be one hell of a coup for Majorca's idea to bolster their limited numbers.

Of course, there were far too many ways for this to backfire. But life in the world of the walking dead was nothing if not exciting and stuffed to exploding with opportunities for serious foul ups. "Hope your head is down, Top," Majorca's voice in Kane's earpiece. "We're coming as fast as the flesh eaters can boogie."

"Roger," Kane said.

"The way you're driving those poor, dead bastards," Valkyrie quipped, "maybe we should be calling *you* top. You have a leather kink to go with that whip cracking hand of yours?"

"Knock it off," Kane snapped, but he smiled at the strange picture that produced in his head.

The recollection of being fifteen and watching cartoons with his jokester pals. Those pals would graduate from jokesters to full on stoners in high school, but back then they were just a bunch of guys who could not control their hormones. One of the cartoons had been a classic sixties Hanna Barbara cheese, featuring a metal masked dude harassing townies by standing astride two lifelike-but-ultimately-robotic sharks. "I'll never forget," one of the hapless teen heroes quips at episode's end, "the sight of that guy riding those two sharks!" Kane's jokester pals had started the laugh-alanche at that little unintentional entendre. Now, he pictured Majorca riding walking dead chicks like a Roman charioteer for the new millennium.

Kane slouched as low as possible, ticking off the seconds in his head. Soon enough, the moaning came. With it, the sounds of shuffling and the rumbling engine of Majorca's ride, a dirt bike scooter pooping just fast enough to keep him ahead of the mob but not so fast that he left them in the dust. Seconds after this came new sounds: the Riders Heaven crowd aspiring for readiness.

The bike passed Kane's position, goosed a little faster to keep dead guy attention, and Kane held his pistol's grip at the ready. No white knuckles. He was safe for the moment, even if the horde decided to descend upon this booth. The door lock worked well enough for him to rip a way into the ceiling, out of reach before they broke through. He did not need a hatch in the roof to take advantage of a ceiling escape.

Automatic rifles opened up at the biker bar, caps popping. It did nothing to lower the moaning. There must've been a hell of a lot of the dead bastards.

"You're doing good, Top." Valkyrie taking Majorca's term of respect. Was he confused, or had she added a little bit of affection? "Shit. You have a straggler, curious for a loaf a'bread or some milk." She pronounced this last as *melk*, like a good local girl.

"Think it's worried there might be a blizzard a'blowing?" he asked.

This was a New England joke from before the world's collapse. The blizzard of '78 was the storm of the century, and forever after any winter storm would be compared to it. During that big blow, the snow fell faster and harder than anticipated, shutting down the northeast for days. People were trapped in their houses or even in cars on the interstate. The ripple effect, in later years, was that at even a hint of a big storm, every grocery store would experience a run on two items: bread and milk. Because snowed in meant French Toast time, Kane supposed.

"You're a stitch, Top." Valkyrie said. "But it's coming into your proximity. Going blazing guns will call the others back to you, so be silent, huh?"

"Sure thing, mom."

From outside the booth, he heard the clatter and clomp of the walking dead's journey around the outer perimeter. That ring held the old refrigerators, all room temperature of course, and the now-empty snack racks once dedicated to single tube style Ritz crackers and red hot chips. The zombie was coming around slowly, like a shopper uncertain of just why he had walked through the door.

Kane slithered across the floor, keeping out of line of sight. He holstered the pistol and produced his knife. With this, he tapped the door's latch, unlocking the bulletproofed portal. Now for another waiting game.

"Top, you aren't going to believe this." Majorca sounding like a kid waking up on December 25th to discover that Santa has made good on the promise to deliver that Darth Vader figure he always wanted. "The goddamn bikers are coming out."

"How many?"

"Uhm," Majorca said, "Looks like all of them to me!"

"What do you mean they're coming out?"

"If they had butterfly nets, they wouldn't look any more ridiculous than they do now."

Of course, they would be emerging from their clubhouse. The sons of bitches would have to be falling in line with the least likely part of the plan at this very moment. When a walking dead bastard was tottering around just out of melee range and he could not risk a headshot from his weapon. There was now no worry about attracting the attention of the dead, but of the living . . .

"Come on, little corpse," he whispered, almost a lullaby singsong, "time to lay down your head."

Clunk, clatter. *Closer*. Not so close that he would risk throwing open the door, however. Not yet—

"She's out, top." Valkyrie telling him the target was outside her armored walls. "The target, I mean." Then, that voice added, "No rush."

Sure, sure. The woman was confounding, all right. As Kane considered a couple of different curses to respond with, the shuffling steps outside his booth came close enough for him to act. He bit his tongue and shoved open the door.

When this sample of the walking dead had been alive, she had been a teenager or possibly early twenties. The number of ragged looking bite marks on her swollen cheeks, bare midriff, arms and shoulders suggested she had not gone easily into that final dark place. The girl had the dark golden complexion that only came from a Brazilian heritage, and her dark hair swung down to the middle of her back. Whatever top she had been wearing was gone, now; a pair of desert style camouflage pants hang from her emaciated frame as though ready to fall off, held up only by a set of protrusive hip bones. As with all the walking dead, time had done her a disservice. Her leathery skin was mostly shriveled tight against her skeletal frame except in a few places where maggots or other unseen vermin bred. In these areas, unnatural lumps and swellings spoke of multigenerational habitation, giving those isolated swollen spots the semblance of an old tenement building that had seen fewer and fewer allotments of maintenance funding over the years. The damage she had sustained glistened the way early scabs did, and fungus colonies ringed the areas like improperly applied eyeliner.

She was not quite two steps away when the zombie's pale blue eyes finally recognized Kane as a living, breathing snack. Her lips peeled back to bare rotted gums and crooked teeth in a halitosis heavy hiss, Kane had stepped in close and brought his blade up under the thing's chin. The tip slammed up through the thing's soft palate, sliced into its hard palate, passed through the nasal cavity and finished its journey in whatever mush occupied the skull. With deft precision, Kane churned the blade handle in vigorous circles, mashing the gray and white matter in wholly dysfunctional ways.

The thing's hands found their way to his shoulders, clenching him and fighting, even as the final death impulse radiated outward from the nervous system. With his free hand, Kane shoved the zombie away, dragging his knife out of the bloodless hole it had cozied up into, and watching the rotter collapse into a stinking heap on the floor.

He counted steady breaths, watching the corpse settle and twitch. This one, at least, was not standing back up again.

A small percentage of the bastards just did not die from the old shoot-them-in-the-head technique; they kept on a'ticking. Whatever son of a bitch had served as Mariner's replacement finger was one such case. The parts continued functioning, seeking out whatever sustenance they could. The first time a walking dead bastard dropped, only to continue pawing its headless way across the room toward the head tapping victor was brown trouser unnerving.

When he reached a ten count, Kane was satisfied enough to turn his back on the thing. He headed to the door, paused to take a SitRep of the outside world, and found that he had somehow ended up in the Twilight Zone.

At Biker Heaven, a group of twenty men and women in biker's leathers and homemade armor were running around the lot either snatching living dead bastards with collars on poles or killing them, seemingly at random. They did not seem to mind the fact that this was dangerous, and when a zombie dropped one of their own number, they stomped both the dropped companion and victorious walking dead bastard without concern. Behind them all, a woman strode along the dive's long front porch, observing, nodding in an approving fashion, and occasionally barking out an order. She was a hell of a specimen of womanity, too. *Good day for it.*

The obvious leader was a stocky thing, not quite six feet tall, with arms like stovepipes. She wore her blonde hair spiky and short, and a white leather patch hid the presumably vacant socket where her left eye had once been. Scars along her face and the slight right-leaning limp suggested she was a survivor of numerous battles. Her leathers were reinforced with football padding around the shoulders, and a steel plate over her chest and stomach. She also had a thing for blades. Kane spotted the handles of no less than five such weapons in her boots, another on her belt and more over her shoulders.

"Hello Catherine Wheels," Kane muttered, studying the scene for any useful intercept routes.

So long as he could get to the Biker Heaven's porch unseen, the big man could take advantage of the commotion to nab the woman, but where would he go? Force her around back and call Majorca to rendezvous with them? That was a recipe for a car chase, since the shock troops would find out what was happening in no time and be on their tails. Force her into the Biker Heaven and force the door shut? He might have a chance to perform a brief interrogation, or he might not, but then what? He would have a horde of ferocious raiders, a plethora of walking dead folks on the other side of the door. That was assuming no one was inside, of course, minding the shop while the others played outside.

Too risky, too bad. The best way to nab her would be to bring in a low flying support and air lift her, which they did not have.

Unless . . . Unless they did not need Catherine Wheels after all.

Kane said, "Valkyrie, do you have Wheels in your sights?"

Valkyrie Force

"Lethality? I can cripple her or drop her. Your choice."

You're good enough to shoot to wound? Kane should not have been surprised, but he found he was anyway. Even the best snipers were trained to shoot to kill. Shooting to wound was a risk that was not worth exploring. "To drop her," he said, "when I give the word."

After two seconds of pause, the response came: "I do now."

"Keep her there," Kane said. "Majorca, get your butt around to this gas station. When I come back whether in a hurry or at a stroll, I want you at a reasonable evac point."

"Affirmative, top. What are you going to do?"

"I'm going to have a chat," Kane said.

He hustled into the street and then ghosted his way past the mob and to the front porch.

Catherine Wheels did not see him until he was almost next to her, pistol aimed for her midsection. "Stay silent or I'll take you now," he said. "Catherine Wheels I presume?"

After uttering a short Farsi curse, Catherine Wheels met him with a steely glare and a sneer. "And just who the nine hells are you supposed to be?"

"I'm the punchline to that distraction," he said.

"Distraction?" Her eye flicked to the side, stealing a glance at the near riot of activity in the parking lot. Though she was trying to stay cool and clear headed, Kane recognized the tells for suspicion. No leader held a throne like this without keeping enemies close.

"Someone believes it's time for a change in leadership," he said.

To her credit, she did not snarl a query about which one of the lot hired him. She muttered, "Well, this is a surprise. Brain is finally making a move, yeah?"

"Brain is poorly named," Kane said. "My boss is getting impatient with excuses, and has authorized me to not stay bought." The key to playing on paranoia was to be just vague enough to keep the target off balance and pointed toward her own enemies, but specific enough on rational reasons to sound good at first brush. When the target found her internal balance and examined the legerdemain, then the trick would fail.

"Is that so?"

"My boss wants scientists. If you tell me where they are, then I can walk out of here."

"That so?" Now she turned to size up Kane, once more.

"And you can do what you like with Brain," he said, bringing her back to her perceived enemy. "Where are the scientists?"

"You want Fowler, yeah?" This was not going well. Her focus was laser beam hot.

"We want the scientists," Kane reiterated. "Brain won't supply answers for our equipment. Brain keeps upping the requests. Is taking him out worth spilling your guts?"

"Maybe I tell you and you kill me anyway, yeah?" she said. "Otherwise how are you expecting to walk out of here?"

"Air lift," Kane snapped.

"Bullshit. No one flies, anymore."

"We do. Talk or I let Brain tell us."

"All I have to do is scream," she said. It was almost a seductive purr.

"And all I have to do is squeeze," he replied indicating the weapon. "The shells will punch through that half inch thick metal plate you're wearing like one of your knives through warm butter."

"We take them east. To Newton." She rattled off coordinates. Military precision. "How's that, tough guy?"

"And where are they kept before you take custody?"

Valkyrie Force

She glanced once more to her horde of biker followers. Maybe weighing calling to them. Kane did not give her a moment's respite. "Three count, now. Where are the scientists before you get them? Three. Two."

Before he got to one, she answered. "There's a facility in Wormtown under a Boylston Street tenement. Dates back to the cold war days. Fowler's interim man holds them there for final transport."

"Thanks," he said, stepping back into the porch's few shadows. The whole conversation had taken less than two minutes.

"You expect me to believe it's that easy, hotshot?" Catherine Wheels sneered like a pro. "You aren't going to kill me, now?"

"Valkyrie, take her home," said Kane before he glided down off the porch and into the mix of bikers and zombies.

Catherine Wheels snarled something that might have been Farsi or might have been orders to her men, raising an arm in a *sieg heil* motion when a hole appeared in the woman's wrist. This haphazard motion alone allowed her the good luck that prevented the bullet driving straight into her cheek, deviating the cartridge to the left and down enough to send it into her collarbone instead. It emerged from the back. A gout of gore splattered across the wall behind her. She swayed on her feet for almost a full second and turned almost a full one hundred eighty degrees away from Kane before gravity had its final say. If she wasn't dead, she was well on her way . . .

After that, the folks in the parking lot took nearly five more seconds to realize that something had happened and then erupt into new activity. The blame game kicked into high gear, and this was followed by some heavy doses of trash talk and brawling. The zombies, forgotten but not gone, rallied as well as they could, and turned the havoc knob from seven to eleven.

Kane slipped from one vehicle to the next, playing that old commando game of dodgem meets parkour known as "if you don't see me, I don't exist." He broke away from the mess and ghosted up the street, while the Hangsaman Boys problem took care of itself.

When he reached Majorca, the small man said, "Nicely done, top."

"This intelligence," Kane said, "still needs to be verified."

"It's enough to get more bodies into our ranks," Majorca observed.

"When you're done with the circle jerk," Valkyrie said over the comm line, "I'll be waiting for you downstairs. Pick me up on the way home?"

"Roger that," Kane said. "Let's get back to civilization, Dougie."

"Affirmative."

Chapter Five

On the ride back, Valkyrie leaned between their seats and said, "You've got balls of solid granite, Kane." Her tone held more affection than accusation. "You took a hell of a chance."

"But the payout was worth it," Kane said. "Now we need to ID this underground facility and these coordinates out in Newton."

"I have an idea for those," she said. "First, there's a guy I know who does information processing with the big super comp on campus. If there is a facility on Boylston street that the war department knew about, then there will be a record somewhere. Even if that record is a shut down authorization or a resupply order from 1975. Old world gov was big on paperwork."

"New world gov," Majorca observed, "is big on nothing."

"They put bodies in the fields," Valkyrie quipped. "And food on their tables."

"They put job-money in our pockets," Kane grumbled in agreement. "If I didn't have work I think I would bust from boredom."

"Not enough wood in the world to sate you?" Valkyrie asked.

Valkyrie Force

It took Kane almost two seconds to register that entendre and the double take that followed it was apparently a good one, the laughing response he got both from his driver and newfound intelligence friend. "Sometimes wood is not enough."

"I hear you," Valkyrie offered a mock sigh. "So much time, so little worthwhile wood."

~*~

The Protective Servicemen and -woman stationed at Checkpoint Nuance were kitted out with night vision and thermal imaging. Useful since they were night's watch. They registered Kane's and his crew half a klick from their vantage point and were ready to receive them. The RFID unit registered the jeep's friendly tag, but due to the hour the Service received them with orange level wariness. Once Kane flashed his authorization, the squad passed the jeep through without another word.

Once Checkpoint Nuance lay behind them and they were again inside the city limits, Kane's mood lightened considerably. There was no more need to worry about pursuit. For the last ten klicks he had been certain someone would be coming for them. Would emerge from the twilight. Apparently the Hangsaman Boys were all hung up over who was responsible and who was next in line.

"Stop by the nearest watering hole and I'll put a bug in my data guy's ear."

Majorca pulled to a stop outside the Tropigala. Once, it had been a dingy nightclub servicing the Hispanic part of the city. Now, it was a dingy nightclub and grill, servicing the sharecropper Hispanic, Brazilian, black and white parts of the city. It was a testament, of sorts, to the oldest truth: No matter how far humanity slunk toward outright destruction, it would never lose the ability to self-hate based off meaningless minutiae like the color of skin a baby was born with or the choice of partners that floated boats/slicked the seas.

Kane studied the dull neon lights gleaming in the encroaching dark. It was only seven o'clock, but the sky was already strongly night hued. "He have a name?" Kane asked, "This magic data man?"

"He does," she said. "And so do I. But since you didn't bother to ask nicely, you don't get to know either one." Then, she did the most mature thing Kane had seen yet. She stuck her tongue out, gave him a raspberry, and then hopped out of the jeep and headed into the bar, shoving past the bouncer with a muttered "*Pedoem-me.*"

Kane clocked a couple of folks packing Saturday Night Special type weapons: cheaply made, mostly homebrewed pistols that were as likely to blow up in the shooter's hand as they were to take an opponent's head off. The worst of the lot held his gaze, doing their damnedest not to turn away, not to blink. "This place feels like trouble," Kane observed.

"Only because you look like law," Majorca said.

"We're dressed the same."

"Yeah, but you're white and you have that brush cut. Me? I blend. These are my people." He poked an elbow toward the lot across the street from the Tropigala. "One street that away is *mi tio.*" Then, he cocked his head toward the rear of the joint. "And one street that way is *mi hermano del sangre.*"

"Blood brother?"

"Yeah," Majorca said, "we were blooded together in Iraq. Then, after the shit hit the fan and the dead started walking, we made it a true brotherhood by getting up this way all the way from Fort Worth."

"You came up from Texas?"

"You bet your ass we did," Majorca said. "And let me tell you something. The ride was seven kinds of hell, but in the end it was worth it."

"Your hermano," Kane said.

"*Hermano.* You're saying it without the Latin flavor, top."

"Hermano," Kane repeated. "He a Protector, too?"

"Nope," Majorca said. He offered Kane a big old smile and added, "I guess the council finished up their Hispanic quota with me. The Injun quota, too. I'm halfsies, after all. One body fills two checkboxes."

"Betcha the Mayor thinks you're a credit to your races," Kane said, and the two of them shared one hell of a laugh.

Valkyrie came out of the joint not three minutes after she went in, hopped into the jeep and said, "Let's roll. All the way to the compound north of UMass."

"Can't he meet us halfway?" Majorca asked. "Gas ain't cheap you know."

"No, he can't. He's the one doing us a favor."

"Right, right." Majorca turned the key and the engine roared alive. He pulled out into the street. Behind them, music kicked on, some saucy salsa.

Valkyrie drummed her fingers on the back of Kane's seat. "You like to go out dancing, big man?"

"Dancing? To music?"

"As opposed to dancing to nothing. Yeah."

"Do I look like a dancer?"

"You'd love it. It's like stomping heads without the gore."

"Maybe in a mosh pit," he said. "But in da club? No thanks."

"You mosh, top?"

"You're giving me grief now too, Majorca?"

"Whatever happened to Dougie? I thought we were on friendlier terms."

"We were until you started helping the enemy ambush me."

"Enemy?" Valkyrie asked. "Ambush? You're a clod, Kane." She shoved back away from his seat with a huff.

Kane shot a glance Majorca's way, and the driver just laughed. "Some folks are clueless," he said, "and some folks don't recognize the clues they've been given."

"You're no help."

~*~

The compound had once been a National Guard facility just up Plantation Street from the University of Massachusetts Medical School. The nondescript brick building was nestled amongst three barbed wire barriers. Alongside it was the motor pool's spillover lot, housing Hummers and two-ton trucks (the infamous deuce and a half model that served as the real winning technology for dubya-dubya-eye-eye, in the last century). The man at the gate entrance buzzed them through once Valkyrie showed her ID. They parked right in front of the main double doors. The building was more inviting inside than out, office space done in military tans and whites. Their contact met them at the entry security desk just inside the brick building.

The data guy rode a wheelchair like a pro, and he had the loose skin of a man who had lost a lot of weight but never quite mastered toning exercises. His pallor was on the corpse gray side, and the sheer amount of sweat he shed gave him a waxy look. His smile was honest enough, filling his gaunt face and adding a twinkle to his warm brown eyes.

"Wheelz," she called him, almost cooing.

The blush that followed this was enough to give him a touch of life. "It is always a pleasure to see you, Sasha," he replied.

She glanced over her shoulder toward Kane and Majorca. "Shucks," she said, "now you know my real name."

Kane filed this away for later. "But I won't use it," he said, "until you invite me to, Valkyrie."

"Plus one to you, big man," she said with a chuckle.

Wheelz looked scared enough to spontaneously pop. "Did I reveal a secret I shouldn't have?"

"Meet my crew of ne'er do wells. This is Majorca. The big man is—"

"Kane," Wheelz and big guy said with a nod. "I know you, sir. Know your work. I've compiled data files."

"Have you, now?" Kane asked. "For whom?"

"Slown," Wheelz said. When Valkyrie offered him a raised eyebrow of surprise, he blushed again and said, "When someone uses whom and who correctly, it gets my guard down." To Majorca, he added, "It's a pleasure to meet you, too."

"I don't think anyone has ever said that to me before," Majorca observed with a wry grin. "Good to know you . . . uhm is it really Wheelz?"

"I'm taking ownership of the handicap," the data guy said, turning his left wheel and then his right, pivoting his body one direction and then the other as though dancing. "I've been this way since the old world. I survived the uprising, I survived McShane and the Invasive Species Incident, and I'll be this way until I die. I figure if no one else takes ownership the mistakes of birth, then I should."

"The what now incident?" Kane asked. That Invasive Species thing was unfamiliar.

"It's been long classified," the data guy replied. To Valkyrie, he said, "Now about this project of yours." It was a hell of a ham-handed segue, but Kane allowed for it. Jacking their jaws about old history – even secret histories that left a bad aftertaste in his curious mouth — would get them nowhere, and this scientist issue was high priority. A regular ticking clock. "I had no idea we had a Sublevel RF in this little burg. Those cold warriors were some crafty motherfuckers. Roll with me."

He turned and sped his way into the complex. Though he looked sickly, he moved with grace and strength. Kane clocked them at about four miles per hour, a healthy gait. They passed closed doors, locked areas, security badges required signs, and finally ended up at a steely gray elevator. Wheelz swiped his personal ID, a light flashed red, and soft hums emerged from the shaft.

Majorca asked, "How long have you known Valkyrie here?"

"It's been, what, about six years now?"

She nodded. "The Mayor had just come to power. And the council."

"McShane was out by then, yeah. The battle fires had died off from the ISI and the Hooligans had made their way west. Yeah, six years. Damn, the time does fly, huh? Have you seen Carruthers lately?" He must have caught a special glance from her because he said, "Well, that's catching up for another day." The elevator door opened. He wheeled in, waited for the others and then thumbed the lowest floor button. The elevator doors closed and descended. "Spooks were paranoid by necessity, in the bad old days of the pre-Glasnost," he said. "I mean there was no telling who was a commie sympathizer, who was a sleeper agent, who was really loyal. A lot of the stuff the various departments dedicated to counterespionage and counter terrorism put in were covert sorts of things. Need to know, deep top secret stuff."

"But you managed to find something for us?" Majorca asked.

"Sasha here knows that I don't brag when I say that I'm the best needle finder ever. No haystack has yet been developed that can stymie my search methods." He glanced toward Kane. "Back in the old world, I was into hackery and then IT security. These days, my skills are not quite in demand for either of those careers. Not until the world gets better, anyway. But for things like this? It's nice to flex those old skillsets." The door opened without a ding or other sound. "Here we are."

A wave of cold air filled the compartment, and Kane realized how long it had been since he had experienced real air conditioning. The room was home to two supercomputers and numerous terminals. The ceiling was a colorful rainbow of Ethernet and miscellaneous other cabling. Test benches bedecked with signal generators, power supplies and numerous other tech goodies filled one wall. Everything was designed for someone on Wheelz' level, except chairs arranged for guests.

"Welcome to my Nervous Center."

"You mean Nerve center, right?" asked Majorca.

"I mean what I said," Wheelz replied with a laugh. "This is the last brain of the old computer world. At least the last one I will ever see. There may be others around. And as such, it's kind of a part – an extension if you will – of my CNS."

"I have never," Kane admitted, "met someone who talks quite as much as you."

"A mile a minute is too slow," Wheelz said. "Long story short, there is a sublevel RF on Boylston street all right. Buried right under one of the apartment buildings over by the Boynton. You know that old place?"

"I know it," Valkyrie said. "The boys might not. They're transplants."

"Lawl," he said, and it took Kane a moment to realize he had just said the verbal equivalent of that old text message L33T speak: LOL. "Anyway, there a multilevel subterranean holding and test facility."

"A what?" Majorca asked. "How could something like that be built without anyone knowing?"

"That's the fun part. In the mid-nineties, there was a hepatitis delta scare, something about the water pipes in the city being so rotten that viruses were breeding in them. The water carried a hepatitis virus strain through the faucets and showerheads of hundreds of people."

"You're kidding me," Majorca said.

"Nope. It happened. You can read up on it." Wheelz tapped away at a keyboard on one of his terminals. "So, that was a great way to move construction materials into the underground areas. It was the way the gubment built a holding facility with a heavy duty virus lab and all sorts of random—"

"Class four?" Kane asked. "What scale are we talking about a class four, here."

"The worst viruses," Valkyrie said. "Herpes. Smallpox. Bubonic plague. The big boys and girls of major death."

"They were experimenting on these things in a populated area like Whoville?" Majorca's complexion had gone a putrid yellow green. "Why would they—?"

"No, no," Wheelz interrupted. "I never found any samples heading their way, just facilities. There was a big bioweapons scare for a while, and I suppose that this bunker was equipped with the facilities to riddle out the answers to big buggy questions."

"Can you get us any kind of floor plans?" Kane asked.

Wheelz filled his cheeks with air as he considered this question and then blew them flat with a flatulent sound to announce he was ready to talk again. "Unfortunately, no. The only plans I can pull up are older than hell. Revision A and tied to original planning. From the stuff I have seen that was dispatched to the lower pits, it looks like the eighties and nineties saw a lot of renovation. Expansion. The front door is in the basement level. About where you'd expect a furnace room to be. Or maybe a storage closet. I'm thinking they converted the old coal storage area into a high security access point."

"What about this facility out by Newton?" Valkyrie asked. "You think there's anything to that?"

"Oh hells yes," Wheelz said. "You bet your patootie there is. Back before our old reliable satellites made earthfall six months ago, I captured some kind of construction going on in Newton. I checked up on the old notes and found they were right at those coordinates."

"Six months ago?" Kane asked. "Why didn't we raid it while it was under construction?"

"I made my report, but you know the Council," Wheelz replied. "Near me is for fearing, further out is forgetabout. Sometimes I miss old man McShane's tyranny. He got things done and had a sense of the bigger picture. Ever since we settled, we've been turning our attentions further and further toward the navel. The Mayor tries to squeak his way in, but he doesn't have the same degrees of freedom that the old man had after the world fell into the crapper."

"Spare me the political speechifying," Kane said. "What is your assessment of the facility?"

"Six months ago, it was being built at a pretty rapid pace. They had lots of labor working it, lots of armed men. I'd say it is a military installation, but not a raider town or anything like that. This had all the makings of something connected to a larger puzzle. This was a cog in a greater machine."

"Fowler," Kane said, and for the first time Wheelz looked empty. "You don't know the bad doctor's work?"

"No," Wheelz said. "Is he one of these humungous wasteland warlord types?"

"He's worse than that," Valkyrie said. "Some say he was a scientist who helped usher in the dead uprising. Some say he's not even from this world completely."

"No shit?" Wheelz asked.

"There's no such thing as devils and demons," Kane said. "Those are metaphors is all."

"I don't know about that," Wheelz replied, and would say no more no matter how Majorca pried. He kept his lips tight like a man who has been burdened with classified knowledge and knows that guns are aimed at his head.

"Be that as it may," Kane said, "we have to operate on facts. Fowler is a threat of the first order. He has pacified cities, gathered raiders under his wings, and has even developed a weird sort of mind control. That last one, he uses on his foot soldiers."

"No shit?"

"Drones are hella bad news," Majorca nodded. "Zombie courage and tenacity, but enough brains to work triggers and employ some tactics."

"That's nightmarish. There was this story I read once, back when I was in high school called 'Wet Work' . . ."

"You tangent too much, Wheelz," Valkyrie said. "I'm going to be riding out to this facility tomorrow, and I'd like to do so with a team. I need a report to give to the Mayor and the council. Something that will get me bodies. Can you do that for me?"

"When do you need it by?" Wheelz asked, eyes slitting with suspicions.

"Ten hundred," she said.

"That's ten ayem?"

"Yes, Wheelz. That's ten ayem."

"Done and done. Come by around eight, we'll share some caff-caff and go over the thing."

Kane blanched at the idea that anyone could drink caff-caff for pleasure. It was a coffee-like concoction, which featured a heavy chalk like aftertaste. He had tried to get an answer about just how it was made, but no one was yet talking.

"You're a doll," Valkyrie said.

To Kane, Wheelz said, "I guess you're dealing with the bunker downtown?"

"Wait," Kane said, "we'll all be going to this compound place."

"Nuh-uh, big man. I ride this one because it's part of my unit's stated principles of purpose. You're Protection Services, and that means keeping home safe."

"Near me is for fearing, further out is forgetabout," Wheelz muttered. He held a folder out to Kane. "This is what you get. It's not all that comprehensive, I'm afraid. But it should get you a bit of support."

Kane accepted the folder and glanced through the contents. Professional looking intelligence report. A few visual aids. Not many pages. "You prepped this already?"

"Sasha's will be done in a couple hours," he said. "But I want a little time to see if I can scrape up some more photo Intel. A compound under construction is easier to see in stages from random photogs we captured and stored on servers than an underground structure that was finished last century would be."

"You have a point," Kane said. He glanced toward Valkyrie. "Want to grab some chow?"

"Why Kane, that's the most romantic invitation I've ever had."

When he realized that Majorca and Wheelz were waiting for their invites, Kane repeated the message to them: "You're all invited too, of course."

"Oh, of course," Majorca said. "But I have a couple of things to do tonight."

Wheelz added, "And my hands are tied for a couple-few hours, but if you could bring me something I'd be ever so grateful."

"Of course," Kane said.

"Oh, of course," Majorca repeated, and there was a snotty, snide quality to his words that Kane could not ignore. "Of *course*."

"Don't listen to them, big guy," Valkyrie said, grabbing his arm and slipping her own into it. "I know you didn't mean it as a date, but a meeting of two . . . appetites."

"Oh jeez, let's just forget the whole—"

"Not on your life, Kane," Valkyrie interrupted. "I finally got you to blush and bluster, don't you ever believe I'm going to let you get away now."

Majorca snickered, Wheelz guffawed, and Kane found himself on an unofficial date with a woman he would not mind officially getting to know better.

Interludes: Bed and Breakfast Stout

It was best that neither of the others decided to make Kane's life more difficult by tagging along. When they ate together, laughed together, teased together and shared three golden moments, there was no one to intrude. When Valkyrie finally acquiesced and allowed him to call her Sasha, and he said it three times as though tasting the word and finding it quite yummy indeed, no one razzed him. When Kane finally got the nerve to invite her back to his place for a nightcap, there was no one to snicker or guffaw. When she accepted, there was no one to make comments.

~*~

When he led her back to the one bedroom apartment he called his own, Kane discovered someone had been there before him. A brown paper bag sat prominently on his table, amidst the clutter of a bachelor's pad. The hanging globe light over that table was buzzing softly, calling special attention to it. The door was not broken open, it had been unlocked with a key, which meant one of three people.

Still, he used caution as he approached the bag. Valkyrie – *Sasha* – giggled at him, but he did not mind. He poked the bag, heard a familiar clink. Peeked inside and found a note sitting atop something.

My stuff is priceless, man.
Keep your worthless chits to yourself
and drink to good health and/with
worthwhile women. – M

"Aw, hell," he said, taking the note out and setting it on the table.

"What did you find?" Sasha asked, sidling up next to him.

He pulled the six pack out, and smiled to himself. Sasha leaned her head against his bicep, and the closeness was a hell of a stimulation. Her touch sent energy coursing through him.

Beneath the note sat a six pack of brown bottles. He pulled the six pack out, withdrew a bottle and Sasha chuckled at the sight. Each had a label Kane had never seen the like of before. "Going Outta Bidness Brew" the beer was called in blocky, cartoonish letters. Along the bottom read: "Kane's Breakfast Stout".

"It's Majorca's last brew batch."

"Duh, big guy. Come on," she said, tugging on his arm. "Let's do a little thirsty-making work. Tomorrow one or both of us may be a'dying."

He turned toward her and their mouths met, and her tongue was a lithe warrior, while his was a steady spearman. The passion between them was hot enough to send sparks sailing toward the ceiling. Her cradled her waist in his hands, and she clung to his neck. After their mouths parted, they gazed into each others eyes for a long, lovely moment. *This is*, he thought, *a hell of a wonderful thing.*

Though she pulled him toward the couch, he dragged her up into his arms. "The bed's better," he said. "I want to share it with you."

They kissed as he carried her down the hallway. She frantically tugged off her shirt, leaving it behind them, marking their trail. In the bedroom, they stripped each other down, and then he drew her into the cool sheets.

They would not stay cool for long. Their mouths played well together, and their bodies even more so. She responded to his every touch, thrust against him even as he thrust into her. She would yield to nothing, and even as she coaxed him to a powerful climax, guiding the way with several of her own, she did not let him rest after he had fired his salvo. She bade him use his mouth on her, and he did so happily. She came one final time, the grand finale for the evening's entertainment, and they spooned afterward.

Kane had never known such a tangle of emotions and the peace that followed.

~*~

Slown received Kane's intelligence report with sputters, starts and disbelief. His office in City Hall's first floor was a smallish affair, dominated by cherry wood furniture, bars over the windows, and even a few tapestries that looked nabbed from the Higgins Medieval History wing of the Worcester Museum of Art. When Valkyrie arrived and showed still more corroborations and extrapolations, the little toad became quick to give them equipment and personnel authorizations.

"I want to see The Mayor," Kane said.

"I am his screen," Slown replied, shutting down the request. "Tell me your plans, and I will see them happen. Depending upon the success of your operation. Operations? Depending upon your success, you will have facetime privileges."

~*~

Valkyrie Force

Sasha's mouth remained full and red, though her body was just as spent and sweaty as her lover's. She said, "Kane, why did you take so long?"

Kane's chapped lips spread into an honest grin as he admired her. Sasha's strong body gleamed in the candle glow. Her blonde hair was mussed from the passionate lovemaking. "I can't help it," he said. "I get so turned on—"

"I didn't mean *that*," she said, swatting him across the cheek. "I meant why did you take so long getting here. Into my life. Why did it take missing scientists and a porn palace snafu to bring us together?"

He considered this, but could think of no response that merited mentioning. He had other things on his mind. "You sure about this plan of yours?"

"It's the only way. You aren't from Newton, and I know the terrain. That means you stay here and find the rat-bastard, while I do the cross-country trek."

She was probably right. Kane hated to admit he was worried about her. The pressure of her success was not all on him, but a good chunk of that pressure was his alone. Providing he intercepted Fowler in time, Sasha and the Away Team would have zero hitches. They were jamming across the countryside, full speed for the compound. Fowler was the key, though. He needed to catch the man before the Away Team got to sighting distance of their target. Should Fowler's people manage to send word, the Away Team's geese were as good as cooked.

He said, "I want you—"

"I want you too, stud."

"I want you," he repeated, "to be careful out there."

"Is the big bad Kane really worried about me?" Her smile had hung on her face for almost ten seconds before it faltered. "What happened to the faith?"

"My faith?"

"I am call sign Valkyrie, right. Flying women on horses from hell. Have a little faith, huh?"

He caressed her cheek and then ran a finger along her jaw. Across her lips. She nibbled his fingertip. He said, "You are a warrior woman."

"Don't forget it, stud." She pinched his nipple. He winced, then smiled. "I like surprising you," she said. "I plan on doing that for a long, long time to come."

When he stopped touching her, he tried to remember the feel of her skin. Just in case he never got the chance to do it again.

Chapter Six

The apartment complex on Boylston Avenue looked innocent enough, despite the intelligence reports citing it as a dead hive. From the street, shapes were visible in the windows—to all appearances, surviving families returning from the chaos of the undead overrun country to a semblance of order in the Worcester safe zone. From his vantage on the tenement's rooftop, Kane appreciated the surreality of those surviving families carrying out ordinary lives like shadow puppets juxtaposed with the Protection Services' Special Weapons and Tactics team massing in the street below.

The radio in his ear hissed for attention, and he pushed it close, unconsciously re-enacting old Secret Service habits—the hardest to break. "Talk to me."

"Status report, Kane," a woman's voice whispered across the com, "Are you in, yet?"

He shivered at this woman's husky purr. Sergeant Margarita Caul was nice enough to look at, but an incomparable joy to listen to. As she was in a command vehicle parked in the street below his position, he could not relish in the first. So, he concentrated on the second.

"We're about to start our descent."

"Lieutenant McCall is prepping for entry." Caul's voice became a sexy purr. "Things are going to get a little manic in short, short order."

"I need fifteen minutes," Kane said. "Buy me that?"

"I'll see what I can do."

As soon as he signed off, Kane dupped fists with his wiry partner. "The clock is ticking, Dougie. You ready?"

"I was born ready, top."

Kane gave a single wave to the zipline team waiting across the street. He got a single ping from a flashlight, which he translated as *Good luck*.

Majorca kicked the roof access door in, and they descended the cramped, mildew-stinking stairs at double time. At the bottom, they found a steel security door—very out of place for a tenement. Kane dared to hope this meant the intel was true: Fowler's secret lab was right here.

"Check out the electronic lock," Majorca said, audibly impressed. His laugh was reminiscent of a seal getting a fish-treat. "Damn near impregnable."

"I don't need to hear that," Kane said.

"You just have to believe, top."

"Faith is a tough thing to come by these days."

"Believe in me, then."

Kane's Desert Eagle automatic pistol filled his hands, the weight a familiar reassurance. Sweat rolled down his ears and brow while Majorca gave the electronic lock his college try best.

"Ten more seconds," Majorca said.

Kane checked his watch. In seven seconds, the SWAT teams would break in. Of course, they were on a different op, though their simple sweep-and-clear would turn into a complete cluster fuck in no time.

Kane said, "We don't have ten."

"Then find enough faith to pray—" The lock popped. "Hell, I only needed five! You see these?" He held up his hands, and his mouth spread in a toothy grin. "Magic is what they are."

Majorca dragged the steel door open, revealing a small guard chamber. Four pasty complexioned men in shiny white helmets and tan uniforms played cards around a small table. They were recovering from the shock of the door opening and grabbed for the rifles leaned against the nearby walls—cards and guns, Kane knew, did not mix.

Kane sighted on one and they all froze. "Where is he?"

None of the men said a word. Kane saw the glaze to their eyes, recognizing the effects of better oblivion through chemistry. Loyalty like this could not be bought, it had to be manufactured. "Take them," Kane said, and Majorca's trank pistol rendered the men useless.

"We're in," Kane reported.

Caul answered with a purr, "Just in time," before the sounds of outrageous violence obliterated any further communications.

Above, the SWAT boys and girls were kicking doors and smashing windows.

Majorca added, "Might want to let the Loot know he can expect hella close quarters. I smelled at least twelve corpses on the way down. These people did not want to give up their dead."

Not that the City Council gave them much reason to cooperate.

Ghettos were by and large insular. Kane knew that was their purpose, keep the minorities packed tight as a powder drum and hope none of them sparked enough to light the others. Powder did not explode, it burned, but when it was packed tight enough there was no appreciable difference—a fire or an explosion could render the veneer of society kaput equally effectively. As the world ended around them, Whoville's surviving power system had regressed seventy years, to the heart of the social inequality movement when the blacks and the Jews and the Chinese were pocketed in separate sectors. Fear of the dead mutated into a full on fear of any others. Gone equality; hello, segregation.

Without trust, there was only schism . . . just like without hope, there was only fear. Worcester's powers kept the ghettos separate and afraid, and it was enough to make a conscientious man sick to the soul. It was truly tragic that humanity could not move past its differences, even on the cusp of the end of the world.

Kane had no patience for that mentality. His handpicked team spanned racial divides. As his grandmother always proclaimed: *from diversity comes strength*. She was a born and raised Cambridge woman, the furthest west she had gone was Newton, and that had been enough. The whole waiting world was well and good, but she was content to let it carry on unseen, filling her life with the neighborhood around her brownstone, which was spitting distance from the Charles. Still, she never bought into the darker skin means stained soul psychopathology of the racists in charge of Order and Law.

Kane dragged the steel door shut behind them. "Make sure no peckerwoods in uniform open this."

"You mean Fowler's guys?" Majorca asked, baring his smoker's yellow teeth in a broad grin, "or the Loot's good ol' boy headbreakers?"

"Either," Kane said. He holstered his pistol, retrieved a rifle, and checked the load. Fowler's boys were using M-14s, oddly old school for such a state of the art operation. The rounds were high grade, though—full metal jackets ready to perpetrate some serious damage.

He thought about Sasha and her Away Team, silently wished them luck, and carried on.

Past the guard room he ventured through a pair of offices, stocked with computers and electronic laboratory equipment he could not identify.

Kane ghosted onward. From the lab, he found himself in a labyrinth of claustrophobically narrow corridors. When he heard voices ahead, he stopped. They weren't approaching. He crept forward for a little recon. He found a grim faced man and woman in lab coats under the glazed but wary eyes of Fowler's goons. Two more drones. Kane recognized the lab coat wearers. They had gone missing from Worcester's Medical Lab.

"Damn it, we've done everything we were supposed to," the fiery-haired woman said. Her name was Trini Brown, and she was an exemplary biochemist who had disappeared after making big strides in developing a neuroblocking agent that could render the dead completely dead. "It's time to let us go. It's time to stop threatening our families."

"Open the door," the other scientist added. He was a gawky looking fellow with a prominent Adam's apple. His name was Leitch. Silas Leitch.

Kane had to get these people back topside. If tomorrow was going to matter, it would be science that saw them through this dark night of the walking wounded.

The M-14 was a semi-automatic rifle. There was no need for him to manually load the next round, as he might with a .30-06 or other hunter's weapon. It would be loud as hell in the enclosed space, however. Once he fired it, everyone in the complex would know he was here. The Desert Eagle pistol, firing one of its .50 cal rounds, would be no quieter. The stopping power for either weapon was unquestionable, though neither was what he would consider a stealthy tool.

Majorca's tranquilizer gun was damn near silent. It was an almost perfect infiltration weapon. Almost. Kane had the real, perfect infiltration weapon on his belt.

He slung the rifle and drew the Emerson CQC-7B knife from its sheath and unfolded the blade. Its 4.6 ounces returned to his hand like an old friend. Of course, he would have to cover the distance before he was spotted.

If Kane'd had more time, he might have taken a uniform from the downed guards. As it was, he would have to find another way.

At about nine feet up, the ceiling was a mess of pipes and wires. Might there be space above that?

He poked his head up, found a good eighteen inches of space and plenty of handholds. Not perfect for a long stretch, but he could use this to get ten feet down a hallway. The knife found its way into a wrist sheath. If he made a fist, two inches of blade would poke past his hand. Punches could pierce, now.

He hefted his weight up, sidled past the colorful network cables and steel encased power lines, and started the short distance, high intensity inching progress along the ceiling. When he found himself overhead, his earpiece chimed. "Door is sealed," Majorca said, "and I'm coming to join you."

Kane replied with a subvocal grunt, and Majorca said, "Roger, top."

It was communication enough. *Join me. Be ready for tangos.*

More argument from below. After ten seconds and his silent prayer that the scientists would not push these men's patience too far, too quickly, Majorca radioed he was in position. "Where are you?"

"I'm to the left," Kane said.

Several things happened simultaneously:

Majorca said, "Roger, top." Dr. Brown said, "I'm leaving." One of the guards said, "Move and I shoot." The other guard said, "What was that?" And Dr. Leitch threw a punch.

Kane dropped from his hold, but his descent was not clean. His shoulder caught on the cables and spun him in midair. His feet connected with the guard who was already reeling from Leitch's blow to the jaw. Leitch, of course, was reeling from the pain in his fist.

Kane's boots collided with the stumbling guard's chest and sent him into the wall. Mid-fall, Kane lashed out toward the other man, whose rifle was pointing at Dr. Brown. This guard was too far for fist or knife.

The drone's finger tightened on the trigger. The M-14's 7.62 mm round would punch a sizeable hole through the unarmored doctor. With the barrel's current position aimed low on her center of mass, the round would likely nail her in the gut, giving her a slow, protracted and painful demise.

A dart appeared in the man's throat, however, and he went over in an instant. Kane landed wrong, but shoved upright. The tango was trying to recover, but Kane leaned in and finished the drone by sliding the blade under his chin, angled up through his soft palate. Kane held the man until he stopped twitching. The killing had been unfortunate but necessary.

"Who," Leitch asked. "Who are *you*?"

Kane ignored this, asking, "How many of you are down here?"

"Two others," Dr. Brown said, remarkably calm for almost getting blown in half. Still, Kane registered her nervousness through a tic: her eyes regularly tracked toward Leitch. The good doctor should never play poker.

"Two?"

"He had Modvi . . . He made an example of her."

Dead, then. That left doctors Prabu and Porter-Goff. "Do you know where Fowler is?"

"He's gone," Leitch said.

Cold terror crept into Kane's heart. "He's what?"

"He said something about a failsafe plan, something about sending a message to Wormtown. I think—"

"The mutagen," Brown said. "He's got a fuck ton of mutagen."

"And what is mutagen?"

She gave him a rundown. Fast details, well explained without being overexplained. By the time she was done, Kane was reeling. A dram of mutagen was way too much. One vial of the colorless toxin added to the water supply would kill the town. Those drinking it would switch sides, from the living to the hungry dead within hours. The lab room he had passed through held at least one hundred vials. "There's more downstairs," she concluded. "A lot more."

"Shit," Majorca said. "No wonder this place is so poorly staffed."

"Majorca, get these two to the exit. We need to make sure they're safe." Kane tapped his earpiece. "Caul? Have the loot get the people out of this building. You hear me?"

Her response came through a hiss of weak signal static. "Impossible," she purred. "These people are dug in tighter than ticks. Here to stay unless forcibly removed. He's playing this one straight from the book. Step by ever-loving step."

"The building is a deathtrap. Possible explosives, possible contagion, possible—" He remembered all the vials of waiting mutagen. How many other vials might be secreted in the place? A sizeable enough blast would send the shit into the atmosphere and make Whoville one more city-tomb in a country – a world – already overflowing with them. "Jesus, hang on." To Majorca, he said, "I have to find this failsafe. Have to deactivate it."

Kane's partner asked, "And the other scientists?"

"Your priority, Majorca. Mine is the city."

"Roger, top."

"I need a layout in ten seconds," Kane said. "Doctors?"

Leitch babbled like a fool. He was useless under pressure. Brown knew her stuff, however. She had a good head, and she provided a breakdown: "The complex is only about seventeen rooms spread over two levels. Our people mostly worked up here."

"And below?"

"Research space and . . . and the dead pits," she said with a shudder. "He would bring the hungry down here. To experiment upon. He kept them in airtight facilities, with recycled mutagen gas running through them."

There it was, Kane thought. Vent the mutagen into the city's air and—

No, that would not work. It might cause some havoc but it would not destroy the city. Would not send a real message other than, "Fowler was here." If Kane knew this lunatic, and from his intense file research, he knew the bastard all too well, Fowler was looking to send a big, big message. Not only to Worcester, but to any city-states in the Disassembled States of America.

"His office?" Kane asked. "Is that below, as well?"

"It is." She gave him walking directions to the elevator and then below. Again, he noted how she looked toward Leitch, who remained oblivious to her glances.

Poor thing must be terrified, Kane thought.

"How do you know all this, Doc?" Majorca asked.

Valkyrie Force

"He wanted to convert me," she said, with obvious distaste, "to his way of thinking. I have a husband, though. I have a family here. I wouldn't give them up, no matter what bennies he tried to offer."

Majorca suddenly tapped his ear and listened. Situational gravity drained the blood from his face. "Just got word from Away Team. They are nearing rendezvous with Big Tango. In three minutes, they're past no-returns."

"Understood," Kane said.

"Do I tell Away to abort?"

"No Dougie. Let them ride on in."

Silence and shock both passed in seconds. Majorca was a professional. "Roger that." Into his earpiece, he relayed Kane's word. "Godspeed," he added afterward. "Come home in one piece."

"Your mission—"

"Civilians first," Majorca said, displeased but resigned. "Locate the bad doctor second."

"Godspeed," Kane said.

"Mr. Kane?"

"Yes, Dr. Brown?"

"Before you go below, grab yourself one of the rebreathers. There are boxes near the elevators and stairs. I think you'll need one."

"Rebreather?"

"To filter gaseous mutagens."

Majorca clasped his partner's shoulder and then offered a knowing smirk. "Don't let Whoville die a horrible death, okay? All my stuff's still here."

Chapter Seven

Sasha frowned at the artistic rendering on the inside of the armored transport's sliding door. A babe with plenty of curves but without eyes. Her defining characteristics were cute little fangs, a bloody machete, latex pants, and stripper shoes.

The personnel transport vehicle rumbled over bad ground, shocks groaning loudly. Sasha caught a roof rail without thinking about it. She had done enough Away missions to know the quirks in this breed of enclosed, armored vehicle. Fuck close quarters, the thing was elbows-in cramped, particularly since so much space was taken up with the drones. The remote controlled killing machines would hopefully not prove necessary, but Kane had insisted they go loaded for bear. Undead, flesh hungry, blood crazed bear.

Larry Gutierrez sidled up nearby. He had an oily way about him that accentuated his natural musk. He was tough and rough, as everyone had to be in this worst of all possible worlds. Though he had little use for "frails" outside the bedroom, Lawrence respected her as more than the useless bit of skin around tits and a pussy.

Larry's lips split in a grin when he saw the artwork. "You like her, bosslady? I think it turned out super stellar, her being such a beauty in an ugly world."

"You did this?"

"You bet."

"Pardon my lack of artistic understanding, but what is she supposed to be?"

"She's you, boss lady." He chuckled. The APC roared over more rocky terrain, and jingled his necklaces—a trio of crosses, one silver, two gold, all gaudy bling. "She's the queen of the wilds, the goddess of blood. She's a vampiress and a goddess and she has no mercy."

"That's what you think of me?"

"That," he laughed, "is what we all *know* of you." He indicated the other men and women in the squad. "We don't have no illusions, Valkyrie. You're queen bitch of this zombie swarmed wasteland."

She perked up at this honorific, stripper shoes or no. "You got that right."

~*~

The Compound was a codename gleaned from coded transmissions the team's communications officer, Toni "Trodes" Harrower, had been intercepting and decrypting for the last seventeen hours. They really had little idea what to expect, but the name's connection to Fowler's weird plans granted it an honorary sinister status. Details were minimal at first. Trodes cracked more, and in time they had map coordinates. It was about a twenty minute drive east of Worcester, midway between the big cities along the Boston Turnpike.

Trodes sat before her comm rig, oversized headphones making her already tiny features looks somehow even more dwarfish. Larry called her the team's Hobbit because she was so tiny—an inch under five feet even and pretty like a classic movie star, with her shoulder length auburn hair and wide anime eyes. However, this rose had thorns—all roses did, if they survived the early days of the rising. The knives in her boots had been bloodied numerous times, and from the crazed look that sometimes came to her eyes, Sasha had to wonder if the blood they had tasted had all come from deaders.

Sasha slid into the seat beside her, motioning the young woman to take the phones off. When Trodes did, Sasha asked, "Any breakthroughs?"

"Some kind of special shipments were dispatched to this Compound," Trodes said. "I still can't figure out just what or if they even came from Wormtown. It's wicked annoying."

That use of wicked as an emphatic was the sure sign of a born Whovillain. Sasha could have laughed. She bit her tongue, however. "It's probably dangerous, yeah?"

"Probably."

"So, we park a distance back and use the drones."

"It's a solid plan, bosslady."

"You see Larry's latest master-pizza?"

"The queen bitch of the wastelands?"

"Yeah."

Trodes glanced toward it. Sasha did too, just in time to see Larry leaning kissably close to the painting. He must have sensed their attention because he reared up, like a kid caught in the act pretending he hadn't been doing anything wrong. It was the stupid human equivalent of a cat washing its tail instead of owning up to its mistakes.

"He's an asshole," Trodes assessed. "But the painting is kick ass."

"You think that's me?"

"That's totally you," Trodes said. "If you were a vampire with a size triple-F cup."

"She does look a little top heavy."

"Larry's no graphic designer," Trodes said. "Not even much of a human being. But he knows how to kick zombie ass."

"That he does."

"I wish we had Big Papi instead."

"I'm surprised the Mayor gave this much," Sasha replied. "Intel was weak, but maybe we made it convincing."

"Yeah, yeah. I know, I know. That doesn't change things any." Trodes jiggled her headphones in a silent request. Sasha let her get back to it.

~*~

Peter Jablonski had made the shift from hack driver to combat driver with little difficulty. He sat behind the APC's wheel with a placid expression and knuckles that didn't look too white.

Sasha slid into shotgun, tugged a map off the dash and studied the front page. "You dip," she said, "this is for Newark!"

"Damn right," he said, showing his Jersey. "Don't you be discounting the pleasures of the Garden State. That place's mother's milk to me."

"What does that even mean?"

He chuckled. "You know what I like about you, boss lady?"

"What's that, Pete?"

"You the one who ain't afraid to call me out on the bee-ess I spew. Most folks would let something like 'That place's mother's milk to me' slide. Not you, no way."

They laughed together for a few seconds. She tossed the map back on the dash. He reached over to restore it to the exact position it had been. The man was a quirky bastard.

"I saw Newark once," she said.

"What'd you think?"

"Looked far away and kind of grimy from the airport windows."

"You were looking from the airport?"

"Yeah."

"That's not Newark," he said. "You have to be in Newark to know her. You have to smell Newark to know her. You have to . . ."

"I was coming back from a conference in Indy," she said. "This was before it all went sour. I was flying back, but my flight got delayed. Then cancelled. I got routed through Newark."

"For Boston?"

"Warwick," she said. "I avoided Logan airport like the plague."

"They routed you through Newark for Rhode Island?"

"And then the plane arrived twenty minutes late. I was stuck in the airport overnight. It was major suck."

"You didn't rent a car? I would've drove." He started reciting the streets, coming up with no less than three possible overland routes to bring her from New Jersey to Massachusetts all complete with estimated travel times. *He must've made one hell of a cabbie*, she thought.

"That's nice and all, but I paid for the plane," she said, "and they stiffed me, saying it wasn't their fault. No refunds if I opted for a rental."

"Major suck," he agreed. "Big time blow."

"You bet," she said. "But you know what? I'd give just about anything to be back there. In that stupid damned airport, shivering from the air conditioning, listening to the Muzak and sipping coffee from Dunkin Donuts. It sucked, but it was civilized suckage."

"I could go for a little prepared coffee myself," he said. "I was more of a Starbucks guy, though. Tall Mocha Frappuccino with whipped cream and chocolate drizzle." He paused to lick his lips, just a quick flick of his tongue across them. "Jesus," he said, "you think we'll ever taste that

Starbucks flavor again? I mean, I tried to replicate it. Added a shot of espresso to my coffee—I had one of those French presses, you know what I mean? Yeah. Make an espresso, then add it to the coffee. It was close but not Starbucks . . . I dream about that flavor sometimes."

She let this hang in the air between them.

"How're we doing?"

"We're almost— *Holy hell!*" The APC had been going through a gentle turn until his ejaculation. Then, he jerked the wheel, performing a hard left. From outside came the sounds of mud hitting the vehicle chassis.

Sasha stared through the windscreen. They had just run into a horde of stationary deaders. The creatures were in the middle of the road, swaying in place. No, she realized, these were not deaders at all. They were dead people, strung up or impaled on spikes and positioned in the road like dolls. Life-sized actionless figures.

Her mind raced with situational analysis, but the meat dolls were too good a distraction. She managed to say, "What on earth?" before the first rocket propelled grenade corkscrewed through the air from an overpass.

"Enemy contact!" she screamed, but Pete was already initiating evasive maneuvers. He gunned the engine and jerked the wheel further left. The vehicle responded to his commands like a trained horse. He rode over the curb, cutting close to a cluster of trees. Asphalt exploded behind them. As he drove, Peter Jablonski muttered, and at first Sasha thought he might be talking to her. Then, she realized what he was saying and to whom: his "You think you can take me? You're messing with the wrong Polack!" commentary was aimed at the hidden attackers.

He cut back across the road when a second RPG launched its shrieking payload toward them. Explosion glow ripped the night apart, and Peter let out a war whoop.

Then something crashed into the APC's rooftop, like the world's biggest flyswatter. This caved some of the steel down, and screams sounded from the rest of the team in the rear compartment.

Something big and cylindrical rolled down the windscreen and under their tires. The vehicle jounced dangerously as it roared over the obstruction. "They smacked us with a tree," Peter said.

"Maybe more than one."

The vehicle's engine was making awful grinding sounds. Peter tried coaxing it, whispering to it as though addressing a lover.

Sasha took this opportunity to check her machine pistol and flip the selector switch to fully automatic. The gun was small enough, unimpressive to the untrained observer. However, it was capable of firing a steady stream of death at whomever she aimed at. The 9mm cartridges did not have the best stopping power or penetration, but enough of them would slow or stop even the most rugged opponent.

The two RPGs fired simultaneously. Peter was good – hell, he was pretty great – but no one was good enough to outmaneuver a pair of launched explosives. To his credit, Peter managed to dodge one.

The other caught them broadside, the warhead blasting a hole through their armor. Screams from the rear, shouts of "Fire in the hole!" and the hiss of an extinguisher doing its damnedest to put out said fire.

A third explosive caught the driver's side front wheel, blowing it to pieces. Peter let out a startled squawk as his console came apart, transforming from automotive components into poor man's antipersonnel mine in no time flat. The detonated console bits exploded outward, ripping bloody furls across Sasha's face and arms, almost blinding her. They tore the driver to pieces.

Heat filled her lungs and stung the backs of her eyes. Sorrow and rage.

Valkyrie Force

In the darkness, the enemy was closing in. Fowler's men. Men from this Compound. They had set an ambush. Somehow, some way they had known that the Away Team was coming. Now they were coming for the survivors. Sasha lifted her machine pistol ready to send the first tango she saw screaming to hell.

They came like the night itself. So many. The windscreens were already blown. Sasha lifted her weapon, held it in both hands, sighted on one of the tangos and put a short burst into him. The tango's arms flailed as it dropped, its weapon clattering to the ground before the owner's corpse joined it.

Good, she thought, already swinging around for the next.

Surprise did not last long. By the time Sasha put a second tango down, the others were scattering for cover or returning fire.

Others from the Team scrambled forward from the APC's burning rear. Larry's shaken voice asked, "What's happening?"

From the corner of her eye, Sasha saw he was carrying a rifle. *Thank god*. "Tangos," she snapped. "From the Compound, most likely. They hit our ride."

"What about Petey?"

"He's." She swallowed the lump. "He's toast. Use your weapon, Larry!"

"I don't need your permission," he said. Then, he raised it and nudged the barrel against her ear.

"The hell?"

"Drop the pistol, boss lady. Don't make me drop you. Fowler has something special for you."

"You . . ." Of course, she realized. The two teams were operating without reports. Autonomous. If Fowler's Compound men knew they were coming, then it was because someone who knew had told them. The chance of bugged briefings was slight. Someone on the team had sold them out. "What's he paying you?"

"All the women I want," Larry said. "Maybe even you, when he's done."

"I'd die before I let you touch me, Larry."

"The queen bitch of the wasteland," he said, voice betraying his honest admiration. His gun barrel insisted she drop her weapon, and to her shame she did. The odds were too bad. Through the window, Larry called, "The Team is pacified!" This received grunts of approval. To her, he added, "I look forward to shagging you in uncomfortable places, boss lady. Maybe I won't use lube." His laughter had never been so derisive. So insulting. "I'm one badass mother, ain't I?" Another jab of his gun barrel insisted she answer.

"You're bad, all right," she said, adding a silent vow to kill him the first chance she got.

A shape appeared in the shattered windshield. A dark gas masked presence. "That her?"

"This is the Away Team's leader. The Valkyrie herself," Larry said.

The new presence pointed an oversized pistol at her.

"Fowler wants her alive," Larry said.

"Alive, yes. Conscious, no." The man shot her. Not a bullet, this was a dart. A trank gun? As the sedative kicked in, dragging her speedily into the dark, she heard the man say, "I hear she's a hellion."

Then, Larry asked, "You think I could, uhm, touch her a bit before we go?"

Rage boiled up, along with the words, "Try it and die, motherfucker," but oblivion welcomed her into its warm embrace before she could hear the masked man's answer.

Chapter Eight

Kane followed Brown's directions through the complex, finding no more waiting drones. He bypassed the elevator for the stairs. In enemy territory, he preferred to trust his own feet instead of a vulnerable cable. He took the steps two at a time, hustling, hustling. At the door to the lower level, he paused to pull on his rebreather.

The device was a redesign of the classic SCUBA getup. A transparent breath mask was designed to cover an adult human's face from forehead to chin, filters would keep the air breathable. If Dr. Trini Brown was to be believed, this would keep him safe should he encounter any mutagen gas. The bad side was, he lost one of his senses. His nose had gotten him through quite a bit before. In the world of the dead, it was one of the most important senses. The dead stank to high heaven, after all. The dead did not seem to smell the living, but the living could sure smell the dead.

At least the unit had a microphone he could jack his headset into. Communication remained possible.

He paused, bracing himself for violence, and then pulled open the door.

Dark passages beyond, broken by occasional spinning yellow emergency lights. Something was wrong down here. The door hinges shrieked a warning as it swung shut behind him.

The corridors were sized to fit three or four people abreast, but the odd lighting and haze made them claustrophobic nightmares. Kane hugged a wall, keeping the M-14 rifle at waist level, aimed forward, alert for contact. His hackles were up, his paranoiac attention to surrounding details set on Overdrive. Doors yawned open on either side of the passage, ahead and behind him. Any of them could vomit up danger.

Compartmentalization kept his trembling under control. He would have to vent the fear later, but for the moment he focused on the task at hand.

Whoville was mother, was father, was home. Without it he would be on the run, again. No better than a scavenger, no better than the other thieves and bandits. This city had given him a purpose, it had given him a code, and it had given him

(*Sasha*)

someone worth fighting for. He would be damned if he was going to lose the place now that he had almost all he could want.

A shape emerged from one of the doorways. Humanoid. The nearest lamp was behind it, and the light cast its features in impenetrable shadow. The second nearest lamp was behind Kane, and his own shadow washed out any hope of identifying the figure.

She stood maybe five-six. Wore a white coat, a dirty shirt and mussed trousers, a pair of comfortable shoes. Her hair was long, matted with sweat or some other liquid. In one hand, she had a gnawed turkey leg. The other curled into a fist.

According to Dr. Brown, no civilians were down here.

Kane put her down, a single 7.62 mm round to the center of mass made a solid punch. Put her on her keister. Too little blood and too little pain response. The shock from such a shot should have put her out. She looked up at him with a childlike curiosity. She was one of the walking dead.

"Sorry," he said, and put a second round through her nose. The back of her head burst, and painted the floor an ugly shade. She flopped over and fell as still as a pacified Injun in a John Wayne western.

He moved over her, shaking his head. The enclosed areas made the gunfire sounds deafening. Still, he had work to do. She had not been dead long, from the decomposition. Still, if she had been interred in one of the dead pits, what was she doing out? If she was one of Dr. Fowler's cronies, why was she walking dead?

Kane's heart hammered.

Something had gone terribly wrong down here. All part of the madman's failsafe plan? Some maniacal Final Solution?

On the wall hung a fire ax and emergency lamp. One of those box lights with a handle on the top. Strong as a floodlight but requiring a free hand to heft.

Kane slung the rifle, pulled his pistol and grabbed the lamp. A cone of illumination revealed more of the passage, but darkened the edges. The doorways were even more impenetrably dark when the light was not trained on them.

Kane hustled. Ahead, he saw placards near the ceiling, which read DP1, DP2, DP3, DP4. *The Dead Pits*. The doors were open. The dead were running around.

The knowledge that he was being followed set his hackles to tingling.

Valkyrie Force

He put his shoulder to solid wall and turned the lamp behind him. Nothing there. No skulking horde of steadily growing shamblers sneaking along behind him. One man amongst a shambling horde? He was beyond vulnerable.

The mutagen gas must be filling the area, too. No sign of this when he came in. No locks on the doors. Anyone, anything could open them. The gas could easily move through an open door, an open vent. Shouldn't there be some kind of safety system in place to prevent this?

Unless *that* was the failsafe plan . . .

Release the gaseous mutagen into the complex. Into the building. When the SWAT team arrives, they breathe it in. They're dead before they know it. They finish their sweep of the building, maybe finish their shift and head off someplace crowded to toss a few brews back. Maybe they even get there before the gas nails them dead and converts them. They won't kill everyone in a bar, but they'll bite one or two. Maybe spread the contagion a little further, a little more.

That's all it would take to kill the city. Wouldn't even take a week. Probably only two, three days tops. This contagion was a nasty, nasty badass biological . . .

"Majorca," he said, "check yourself for . . ." Feedback whined, loud as a baby shrieking in his ear. "Majorca?" No good. Damn it. Something in the construction was preventing communication. Too much concrete, too much . . . He had to abort. Get topside or clear enough to warn . . .

Movement down the passageway back the way he had come. Shadows dancing in the rotating yellow emergency lamps. Dozens of them, but Kane could not say for sure how many actual shamblers. No going back. Not that way and not now. He hurried deeper into this labyrinthine complex, praying that even Doctor Fowler would not be the sort of lunatic to unleash total Hell upon the city. The mind capable of that level of monstrosity was not simply beyond rational but one step into outright alien. The Nazis were not so ruthless to kill everyone—sure, Kane conceded, they did their best to wipe out Jews and queers and gypsies, but that was to make room for good old Germans. Who would inherit the earth after Fowler was done?

No time to worry about that.

Kane hustled forward, ducked into the nearest doorway. Best to make the enemy bottleneck. It was as close as he could get to a Thermopylae defensive position.

The Dead Pit was an apt name for this zombie fishbowl. A sixty meter diameter tank, the floor a gently declining bowl. Above, a window looking in from the first floor. Down where Kane stood, rotted remnants of half disintegrated and half devoured bodies littered the blood and mud splotched floor. Whatever gore pond had collected in the room's lowest point was gone, drained through grating and shredded steel panels. The dead had certainly been hard at work here, tearing up the steel plating to get at the ground beneath. What about nature called so strongly to these shamblers?

The first of the walking dead staggered past the Dead Pit. Kane trained his rifle on the doorway. It did not pause, kept going. A power walker who didn't know when to quit.

Kane remained tense, the rifle filling his hands. An itch on his wrist, he realized was just an itch in his mind—what time is it, what time is it? A question on repeat, endlessly playing in the iPod of his thoughts. Distracting. Sasha was beyond the point of no return. She and her team would have to take care of themselves.

He had a city to worry about.

He had—

Valkyrie Force

Two more examples of the walking dead appeared, pausing in the doorway. Their faces were puffy and yellow, eyes glazed and wide, ruptured sores draining pus down foreheads and cheeks. Their clothes were civilian scientists—jeans and business casual polo shirts under white coats. Their mouths were circled with blood. One's cheekbone was visible through tattered facial meat.

Kane wished them onward, hoping they would follow the power walker. As one, they turned toward him. All that was human about them vanished when they snarled. Kane turned his rifle on the nearest of the lot and squeezed his trigger. The weapon bucked. Its round caught this tango in the lower jaw, blowing through putrescent meat and brittle bone. The cartridge must have deformed when it blasted through the bone. Instead of blowing through the skull, the round bounced around inside, rattling like a broken bell inside a shaken cat toy. The deader dropped to its knees, its mind minced.

Kane brought the rifle around, as the second deader surged forward. His M14 barked, and the deader fell aside, struggling to rise. Shoulder blown to hell, but its head still intact.

Kane put the rifle's butt to his shoulder, and sighted down the barrel. The weapon bucked, and the deader stopped struggling.

A fourth deader was already on the move through the doorway. A woman whose bowels had been torn open. Her lone remaining breast bobbed like a meat yo-yo as she clawed at Kane's face. He shrugged aside, grateful for the mask to protect his eyes. The rifle came around, wooden stock shifting into a club's role. He batted her in the face, and left an indentation in the soft pulp. She stumbled back, her skull broken. Her eyes now turned slightly toward each other in a comic expression, gazing over the gap that was her nose. A nose that now decorated the rifle's stock.

Kane turned the barrel toward her, now. Squeezed when it was under her chin. Her head vanished, her feet slipped in the gore decorating the floor, and a perfect pratfall dropped her in place. The nose dropped from the rifle stock with a final soft splat.

His stomach filled his throat. Cordite and raw earth and old blood and rotten meat mixed into a disgusting reek. It was then he realized his mask had been breached.

Calm vanished beneath a panic tsunami.

He held his breath, though this was pointless—he would have to breathe eventually. Tears filled his eyes, and the ugly flavor of bile coated his tongue. More dead came through the doorway, into the pit.

His rifle bucked three more times, and two bodies hit the floor. Empty. He dropped it, drew his pistol in time for the eternal power walker to return. It pawed its fallen companions like an overzealous gym teacher—Kane envisioned an R. Lee Ermey type voice accompanying the paws and tugs, saying "Get up you maggot heads! I don't remember giving you permission to lie down!"

"Permission granted," Kane said, and he squeezed his trigger.

It would have been one shot one kill, had a screaming something not smashed through the window above and somersaulted through the air. That screaming something, Kane discovered, was Majorca.

A woman's shrieks followed him down—agonized, terrified sounds. Dr. Brown? Wet sounds brought an end to these shrieks. The distinct splatter sounds of a body being torn to pieces.

The distraction kicked Kane's aim off. His Desert Eagle punched a hole through the wall.

The power walking deader did not glance toward the source of the gunshot, it charged. Moving with more purpose than Kane believed possible, it barreled into him, clawing and biting and tearing at him. Its fingers were curled, hands becoming crude but effective claws. His pistol vanished into the scum. Kane shoved at this attacking creature, but it clung fast.

Kane grappled with the thing, keeping it from chomping flesh. When he could, he struggled to fetch the Emerson CQC-7B from his belt. The thing snarled at the blade, as though it were a sentient adversary, a rival predator trespassing on marked territory.

Kane rolled over so he was atop the creature. Shoved the blade toward the deader's face. His blade stopped inches from payoff. The damned thing had caught his wrist. Strong. Kane clapped both hands on the pommel, clasping them as though offering prayer, and forced his hands down. Adrenaline kicked in, doubling his strength. The knife tip reflected in the thing's glazed eye before it slammed through the *os* lacrimale and into the eye socket. With a twist, he started the lobotomy process. The thing actually screamed before he finished the job.

Zombies didn't scream.

A chill crawled up Kane's spine. The rules he had been comfortable with were all gone out the window now. What the hell was happening?

A groan from the collapsed heap. After retrieving his pistol, Kane pulled Majorca over. Blood oozed from scratches. His eyes were a bloodshot mess. He was turning. Damn it all, Majorca was already coming back. Kane whispered apologies as he brought his Desert Eagle under the man's chin. One squeeze and that would spell the end.

"Wait. Kane, please."

"I'm here," Kane said.

"I'll be okay. I—" He tried to move, but something in his back snapped and he let out a string of curses. "I'm done. Aren't I? No walking home for me."

"You're walking wounded," Kane said. It was one step removed from walking dead.

"Oh Kane," Majorca whispered. "Don't let me die down here. Not in this evil place. My soul . . ."

"What about your soul?"

"It won't find its way out. Don't let me wander around down here. Not in this darkness. Bring me to the air, bring me to the light."

"You won't rot down here," Kane said. "I promise."

"Leitch," he said, "led us into a trap. A room flooded with gas. He was . . . He was *masquerading*."

"What?"

"A deader," Majorca said. "But who acts like one of us."

Was it possible? The walking dead were pretty obvious, when they got up close. They looked like dazed, shell shocked folks from afar, but in your face everything human vanished, and there was only ravenous monster. Kane had to admit the idea of a deader that could remain a victim of the hunger without being mindlessly enslaved was pretty horrifying.

You couldn't hate a zombie. Not really. Like tigers and hyenas, they were just driven to *do, to be*. A cannibal, however, chose his course of actions. Whether it was alive or undead, you could not help but hate something that *chose* to eat you.

"Oh God, Kane. It hurts. I'm cold and empty but the . . . the darkness is *alive*. It's twisting inside me. Writhing down in my stomach, in my head. It hurts, hurts, *hurts*." Blood and tears rolled down Majorca's face. Death tremors had come to his hands early. His feet. "Don't leave me here."

"I'm sorry, Dougie."

Valkyrie Force

Majorca's eyes pinched shut, and a stream of blasphemy flowed from his lips. This was how a man's faith could be shattered. Kane endured the verbal assault until his partner's slurred words became whimpers.

Then, he squeezed his trigger.

Then, he whispered: "God. Please take Douglas Majorca from this place. He has served you well. Deliver him from this evil." He did not expect this prayer to find God's ear. The Principle Urge, he had long ago decided, could be the biggest bastard in all creation.

Kane carried the dead man to the doorway.

The sounds of approaching dead echoed from all sides. They were coming, now. Coming in droves. He did not have ammunition enough to survive an onslaught. He could not stab an army to death either. To Majorca, he said, "I'm sorry friend."

Majorca's eyes accused when Kane leaned him against the wall—Kane promised to return for him. If he survived to escape, that was.

Chapter Nine

When Sasha came around, she was tied to a chair in a padded cell. She was not wearing her combat armor or fatigues. Instead, she wore a one-size-fits-none blue fabric hospital gown. She could smell her own sweat and . . . was that urine? How long had she been out? It could not have been long, could it?

Two minutes after she woke, a door opened. In came a stern faced man with a scar between his nose and lips. "Glad to see you're awake," he said. His voice was that of the man who tranked her.

"You're not Fowler," she said.

"No," he admitted, "I'm the man in charge of The Compound."

"What man in charge enters a hot zone?"

"This man does," he said. He leaned in to study her face. "Woundwort is my call sign. I lead my men from the front instead of the rear."

Curious choice for a code name. "What kind of name is Woundwort?"

"A general's," he said. "And it is mine, as yours is Valkyrie."

"We're in the Compound, aren't we?"

"We are."

"And what is this place all about?"

"Actually, I ask the questions," he said with a ghost of a smile. "If you don't mind."

"I do mind," she said. "I want answers."

"I have not yet permitted Gutierrez to rape you," Woundwort said. "But my graces will not remain quite so good if you remain obstreperous."

The threat should not have had quite the effect it did. She was trembling, and cursing herself for this response.

"There's a good girl."

She bit back her vulgar retort. The idea of Larry . . . touching her . . . was too much, too strong, too terrifying. *Damn it,* she chastised herself, *cowgirl up! He's just mucking with your head! Psyching you out!*

"I want to know everything you can tell me about Worcester's civilian population."

"What?"

"You heard me."

"What do you want with them?"

"Are they clustered together? Are they content?" That scar made his sneer was the stuff of nightmares. "We've heard stories about inequality and . . . fomenting revolution."

"So, Gutierrez isn't a good enough information source? His attention too fixed on the things he can screw instead of the intel you can use?" In a bizarre non sequitur, she realized that last part almost rhymed.

"He's told us plenty," Woundwort said. "I want to hear verification from you, so I know I can trust you. If I trust you, I might see clear to calling the beasts off of you. Welcoming you into our little Compound.

We're on the bleeding edge, here. Paving the way to a beautiful new world."

"You sound just like the high fallutin' brainiacs who were responsible for the worst of the old world. Even worse than this zombie land we live in."

"Do I, indeed?" He stepped away and then turned his back to her. She envisioned the dagger she wanted to slip between his sixth and seventh ribs, right in the sweet spot that would stop his heart instantly. "I want to know about Worcester," he said.

"Stop by our travel bureau," she quipped. "They're friendly and knowledgeable chappies and chicks. Great place to raise kids."

"You'll tell me what I want, eventually."

"If you let that son of a bitch loose on me, I'll kill him. Tied down or not, I'll kill him."

"And what if I turn him on someone else?" With a tilt of his head, the door opened again. There must be a hidden camera in here, she thought. Two grunts in UN uniforms dragged a new chair in. Bound to it: a ball-gagged Toni "Trodes" Harrower.

"I'm sure if we offered him an alternative," Woundwort said, "to play with in front of you, of course, our little mole would be quite content."

Cold horror drained Sasha's resistance.

"Now, will you answer my questions?"

She could say nothing. Her eyes locked on Trodes, surveying the damage. Someone had beaten the small woman. A bandage and tape covered one cheek, doing nothing to hide the puffiness around the eyes or the abrasion on her forehead.

You bastards, Sasha thought. *You monsters. You're worse than any shambler. Worse than any deader.*

"My patience wears thin," Woundwort said.

"I don't know anything!"

"You know enough," Woundwort said. To Trodes he said, "Your leader here does not answer me, though she knows the price her ignorance has. She knows you will be hurt in the most creative ways, yet still she remains obstinate." Trodes gaze fixed on Sasha now.

To the open door, Woundwort called, "You may come in."

Larry strutted through the door, his grin wide and feral. "The waif is yours," Woundwort said. "To do with as you wish."

"Stop this, Woundwort!" Sasha screamed, but the men ignored her.

Larry drew a combat knife from his belt and pointed it toward Sasha. "What about her?"

"Not yet," Woundwort said. "But she must watch and listen to what you do."

"Never had an audience before."

"What man doesn't want a lovely, helpless woman watching him break in another?"

"This is the best Christmas present I ever got!" Larry clapped his hands like a trained seal. The combat knife wobbled in his grip, and Sasha hoped he might drop it. Stab himself in the foot or some major artery. No luck.

Woundwort's lips stretched into an evil leer. "I'll leave you to it." Then, he walked out, his boots serving up a slow applause for the coming spectacle.

After the door clapped shut, Larry said, "Might as well get to it." He shoved Trodes' chair forward. "Fanny up," he said. "Just the way I like them!"

Trodes was breathing quickly, panicking. Sasha could smell her fear.

Larry's laughter could have made a jackal sound endearing. "Are you peeing yourself, girlie? Think that'll ward me off? I hate to disappoint you, but I got needs a little urine won't stop." To Sasha he said, "Watch me, now."

Larry spun the knife around his finger, doing for the weapon what a showy gunslinger did for pistols. Then, he sliced through the ropes holding Trodes to the chair. "This thing is so sharp and sweet," he said. "I got plans for it."

For now, the plan involved stabbing it into the cushioned floor so he could tug down Trodes' pants. He dragged them to her knees.

"White cotton," he said. "How boring."

If Sasha could get loose, she would . . . she'd . . . She tugged and squirmed and shifted and nothing helped. Nothing.

Then, she noticed something that brought a flutter to her heart. Trodes' hands were free. The knife had been sharper than Larry had expected or, more likely, he had been sloppy with his cutting. He had maybe sliced into ropes he had not intended to. If his attention remained fixated on Trodes, Sasha knew, she would not be able to do anything with her freedom, but if he could be distracted . . .

"Larry," Sasha said, trying to sound sweet. To sound alluring. She hated herself for this. "Oh Larry, will you do something for me?"

He looked toward her, jaw dropped, eyes wide with lust.

"I know you like me," Sasha said. "Know you want me. Will you show me your big strong thing? I . . . I want to see it." He seemed hesitant. "Please show me?" She licked her lips and watched his hesitation vanish.

"You bet!" He stood up, ignoring his other victim for the moment. She knew what was running through his mind, it was obvious: His prize, the bitch queen of the wasteland, was gracing him by playing out his fantasy.

He dropped trou, and Sasha beheld the mightiness. She laughed at what she saw. Guffawed.

His features contorted with rage. "What are you *laughing* at?"

Trodes took advantage of the moment. Caught the knife's hilt. In one motion, she ripped the blade from the floor and jabbed it into Larry's exposed groin. He shrieked, voice kicking up an octave. Trodes twisted the knife, then did a trick with her wrist that brought the blade out and around. Severed meat plopped to the floor two seconds before Larry dropped. He clawed at his crotch as though he might be able to stop the blood. To erase the dismemberment by hiding it in his palms.

Trodes did not give the wanna-be rapist long to recover. She slit his throat. As he died, she hurried to free Sasha. They left bonds and gag atop Larry's cooling corpse like decorations on a macabre tannenbaum.

The shut door was a taunt and a terror. Sasha found herself wondering, *When will it open? How long before more turtleheads come squirting through?*

When Sasha was free, Trodes allowed herself a shiver. Sasha let her have the moment without contact. If she wanted or needed another, Trodes would ask. Only a stupid man would assume a shivering woman was afraid or weak or otherwise in need of coddling or carrying. Sometimes a person just needed to shake the effects away.

Sasha watched that door, ever wary for signs of Woundwort's oncoming army.

After twenty or thirty seconds, Trodes said, "There're worse things out there than hungry dead, aren't there? Way worse."

"There are."

Trodes laughed, and Sasha had never heard a more scornful sound. "I shouldn't be surprised. I really shouldn't. I'm no stranger to human awfulness." The laughter returned, three quick barks. "But I *am* surprised. Stupid me, huh? My brain is screaming: 'How could this happen to me again?' I mean the world ended, right? That world . . . the place where that behavior came from . . . it should be dead, too. Rotting on the vine. That mentality should be gone. We're on the brink of extinction, here! What the hell is wrong with people?"

"The same things that have been wrong since the beginning," Sasha said. "There will always be monsters among us. We've survived them this long, we'll keep on surviving."

"I hate men," Trodes said. Her already white-knuckled grip on the knife tightened until those knuckles cracked.

Sasha said nothing because there was nothing to say. *Not all men are like that?* Too trite. *Larry was no man?* Too dismissive and ultimately unhelpful. In fact, it was probably best to let Trodes hate for a while. Hate kept a body going, kept the will focused. Trodes would come around in her own time, or she wouldn't. That decision was out of Sasha's hands.

"Think there are keys in here?"

"Probably not," Trodes said, "unless these guys are real idiots."

"They all won't be," Sasha said, "but we don't need them to be. We just need one irredeemable moron."

A quick check of his pockets showed Larry may well be that moron.

"Do you think they'll open this door?" Trodes asked.

"Only one way to find out," Sasha said. "Let's pray: Please let Larry be the moron we need." They both repeated this prayer as Sasha stabbed one key after another into the lock tried to twist and found it wasn't right.

On the fourth of five tries, Providence or pure chance granted them their wish. The door's lock clicked open.

~*~

Outside the cell was a long hallways, lined with similar security doors. No telling if there were other prisoners waiting inside the rooms beyond.

"We can't just leave," Trodes said. "That's be abandoning anyone caught in these rooms."

"Maybe there's a list of prisoners somewhere," Sasha said. "We can't push our luck by checking these one at a time. I see lights up that way. Maybe a monitoring station?"

"I hope those cameras are not working," Trodes said, indicating a pair of dark shapes near the ceiling.

Sasha said, "Let's go before the men with shotguns show up."

They ghosted up the hallway. Trodes no longer held the knife in a tight grip. Training returned, loosening her fingers. She held the knife low, ready to strike. Sasha kept her hands curled by open, ready to deliver a jab or slash to an enemy's sensitive places. No one stopped their progress.

The lights came from bank of monitors. Two men in uniforms were parked behind it, masks hung to one side, rifles leaned against walls. They were trading the worst jokes Sasha had ever heard, but laughing like they were world class humorists.

Sasha and Trodes split up, moving around either side of the computer bank. At Sasha's hissed command, the two women struck. Controlled knife slashes and martial art strikes left the punch line to "Why are women like dog turds?" unuttered. One man struggled to breathe through a gore gushing throat, dying while his companion lay sprawled on the floor twitching with a broken neck.

"Good riddance," Trodes said.

After picking up an assault rifle and checking the chamber—it was loaded and ready to rock—Sasha studied the bank of monitors. Six were dedicated to security cameras, switching between images from at least two dozen cameras. A fifth monitor was connected to some kind of Compound computer system. "Think any of these might be useful?"

"The server connection might," she said. "If we could gain access."

Almost on cue, the sound of a toilet flushed from beyond a nearby door. Seconds later the door opened, and a third guard emerged, adjusting the crotch of his BDUs. He stared at the two women with gap-jawed disbelief. Then he saw the weapon in Sasha's hands, the muzzle of which was pointed just below his guts. "Shee-it," he said, expressing good-old-boy surprise with authority.

"Hands up," Sasha said.

The man's nametag read Slick. "Damn, girl. You know how to even use that—" His words failed when she switched the weapon from single fire to full auto with a trained flick of her thumb. "I guess you do."

Trodes asked, "You know the password to access this system?"

"You talking to me?"

"No, the redneck behind you," Trodes snapped, and he almost turned around. "I think he's useless, Valkyrie."

Sasha considered him, then nodded. "Alright, we waste him."

"Wait! I . . . I know a couple of the passcodes, sure!"

Trodes slid into the seat before the keyboard and poised her fingers to tap as urged. "Start reciting."

Slick spoke slowly, well aware his life depended on careful and precise answers.

"Looks like there're no other prisoners, boss lady," Trodes said.

Sasha thought about the five others in the APC. "The team?"

"They aren't here. Maybe they got away during the confusion or never made it out of the wreck."

Sasha did a bit more exploration, gliding through security walls with ease. Before the world had ended Trodes had been a computer security expert. Sasha now wondered what side of security she had worked, then thought *Thank God she's on our side.*

After a few minutes, Sasha said, "Jesus. This Compound is just one of a ring of Compounds, which each have uplinks to Fowler's personal headquarters. It's a complex system. Compounds stand between Fowler and sleeper cells or secret lab setups in survivor enclaves across the country." After some more typing and hacking, she said, "Fowler's been controlling communications—blocking them. He's been . . . doing some terrible, terrible stuff. But he's been working multiple angles, several fronts."

"Like what?"

"Toxin to kill one zone, then antidote to inoculate his own troops so they could move in after the earth was scorched."

"Can you get us all that material?" Sasha asked.

"Sure," she said.

"And then we get the Hell out of here," Sasha said.

"Drop it," Slick ordered. While they had been distracted, the man had found a pistol and was pointing it between them. The message was a simple one: *I'll shoot whomever I have to*. With a disgusting leer, he added, "Not like you were going to use that peashooter anyway."

Sasha used her peashooter. The burst almost ripped the guard in half. He did not even have time to look surprised before he pitched backward. The gunfire was loud enough to wake whatever dead weren't already walking the earth.

"Can you get us a way out of here?"

"They are all set to shut on lockdown," Trodes said. "Damn it! The process has begun."

"Any ideas?"

"Actually yes."

"What's that?"

"Woundwort's office," Trodes said. She tapped some more, pulled up maps. "It's not far away."

"Oh really?"

~*~

The Compound was mobilizing, and it was doing so at a goodly speed. However, no security protocol was perfect. No matter how powerful a spotlight was, its sweep patterns left plenty of shadows. Sasha and Trodes flitted through the darkness, the chinks in the system.

Woundwort's office turned out to be a Spartan space with only a single unnecessary adornment. This touch of personality was a vintage poster, featuring a blonde haired dominatrix wielding a riding crop and wearing a World War II uniform. It was a movie Sasha had never heard of. Something called *Ilsa: She Wolf of the SS*.

Woundwort was hanging up the phone when they came in, rifles trained on him. He frowned. "You two?"

"Surprised?"

"You're more capable than any women I have ever known," he admitted. "And resourceful. I'm surprised."

Sasha asked, "You're in charge here?"

"I am," he said. "But once security lockdown has begun, there is no stopping them until deactivated from off site."

Trodes said, "So call your gatekeepers."

"Impossible," he said. "This little capture sequence is entirely what that protocol is intended to circumvent."

"What's your back door?" Sasha asked.

"My . . ."

"You're a monster, but you're also a smart man, Woundwort," Sasha said. "You might go into the field with your men, but you're a survivor.

You wouldn't be stuck without a back door. I mean what if the deaders breached the walls? You'd want a way out."

"Wow, you just turned gray as the grave, Woundwort," Trodes said.

Sasha said, "That means I hit the nail on the head, right?"

He licked his lips, looking close to fainting. "I may have a way out. How do I know you won't kill me?"

"You don't," Sasha said.

"Well, if I'm to die, then I prefer to do it here. I won't tell you anything."

"If I guarantee you we'll let you go?"

"You know I'll come after you later," he said. "There's no way you will let me live. I wouldn't."

"That's where we differ. I prefer to keep my word," Sasha said, "and you prefer to get what you want."

"Give him a couple minutes to consider his options," Trodes said. "I want to fuck around with his computer. It's probably got better access."

Sasha enjoyed watching the man's eyes widening. She liked his fear. With a tilt of her head, Sasha directed Woundwort's attention to a nearby chair. "Park it and think. You have maybe five minutes to decide." She already knew what he was going to say. His agreement to her terms was in the way his shoulders slumped, in his bloodless complexion, his self-pitying and self-loathing frown.

Trodes sat down and said, "*All right.*" Sasha took this as a good sign. When Trodes said, "Time to hack Fowler's whole world," Sasha allowed herself to smile.

She decided to give Woundwort seven minutes.

His answer did not surprise her.

Chapter Ten

In the complex's nightmarish hallway, with heavy heart and light head, Kane stumbled onward.

The next deader he found was a round woman with square glasses and a savaged throat. Not a scientist, this was some citizen who had been dead long enough to go green and bloated. He put a cartridge above her nose, and her rotten brains speckled the wall in black globs. His grief wanted him to squeeze again. And again. And again. Just transform this walking dead thing into paste.

It was grief.

Kane bit down on it, like the pin of a grenade. One jerk of his head and the rage would overwhelm. He kept it locked down tight, however. He remained in control.

Further down, he found a computer room and locked himself inside. Half a dozen monitors flashed password authentication requests. Machines locked down. Around the walls, nonfunctioning cooling equipment and several large, unmarked tanks. These, Kane supposed, were not filled with laughing gas but something more toxic.

Valkyrie Force

On the floor lay a sprawled body in T-shirt, SWAT pants, and Doc Martins. A pair of glasses—the thick dark frames Kane associated with Buddy Holly—lay crushed on the floor nearby. The dead man had been a round bodied fellow, thinning hair. Shaped like Ron Howard's brother, the character actor who played a lot of trolls in z-grade flicks. No deader jaws had found this body. A nasty pair of holes opened on a tunnel through his gray matter; the larger of these was above the corpse's left eye. Not self inflicted, then. This guy had been tapped in the back of the head.

He patted the guy down, found a wallet with someone else's driver's license and family pictures in his back pocket and a crushed envelope addressed to Kane in the corpse's left cargo pocket. Inside the last, a letter.

Dearest Kane,

If you've made it this far, then you're a very lucky man. However, not lucky enough to catch me!

Fare thee well. Fare thee nice. I wish I may I wish I might see your fucking face tonight as the city falls to pieces around you. Hope your evenings are entertaining, and your death is slow, painful, and long after those you love have all died in the most excruciating fashion possible.

Ta,

Dr. F

BTW: Oh, wait! I CAN see your face. Look up and say cheese!

Kane glanced up from the corpse, found a small webcam pointed down at him. Past that, in the room's corner, a security camera hung in such a position to catch most or the computer room. One of these was transmitting images to the bad doctor. Kane did not bother to say, *Cheese.* Let the bastard take that how he liked.

Kane scowled and tossed the letter aside.

Then, he studied the computers. He was no hacker. The skill of opening locks was Majorca's forte. Kane stewed for a moment, typed

FOWLER, and got an Incorrect Password message. He typed his own name, KANE, and got another Incorrect Password message.

At least Fowler was not predictable, then.

He studied the room's layout. No escape routes other than the door he'd locked. A pair of vents were large enough for him to squeeze his head through, but not his shoulders. He was caught.

A soft sound at the door sent a chill up his spine. Scratching nails. A walking dead out there. Where there was one, there would be more.

His head was warm, sweat trickled down his neck.

Why had he locked himself in here? What did he hope to accomplish?

He glared at the cameras, and found himself wishing Fowler were in the room with him. Just for five minutes. One would be enough to wring the scrawny man's throat, but five would give Kane a chance to lay down some serious pain. Five would let him . . . "Calm down, soldier."

He wiped a hand across his head, found a thin sheen of grimy sweat. How much longer did he have for this world? How—?

Upstairs. Leitch was up there. The walking dead man masquerading as a living member of Whoville society. When the team working the building did not hear from Kane, they would come down. They would save whomever they could.

He almost clapped his palm against his forehead. *Brown had been trying to warn him about Leitch.* She had not come out and said something—why? Because she was being watched? Scrutinized by something she felt she could trick through verbal subterfuge?

Leitch was Fowler's plan. Get a masquerader out of this building, and he would be whisked away for debriefing. The city's top men would want to talk with him, and that would give him a chance to . . . do something to them. Convert them into smart dead? What would that accomplish, unless Leitch had some kind of control over the dead he made—like the mythical bloodsucker Dracula had over his creations. Say Leitch became a puppet master, a zombie master over the deaders. They would serve him.

Furthermore, say Leitch himself was under the direct control of . . .

Kane cursed to himself. It made a kind of sense. Psychopathic sense, anyway.

Fowler could waltz into Worcester as its defacto leader. Or he could wipe it off the map, all by pulling the strings of a deader puppet master.

There were too many variables. How could he hope to make good on this?

Fowler was insane, but was he *that far* off his nut?

Even if Leitch failed to infect all the city's elite, he could . . . Could get enough of them, couldn't he?

"Why didn't I see it? Why didn't I *realize*?" Kane had to get out of here. He had to catch up to Leitch and put a bullet in his brainpan.

More scratching at the door. The zombies outside were playing at being impatient cats. Kane checked his pistol. Full clip. One more clip after this and then he was down to combat knife and teeth.

He worked out a battle plan: get through the door, make for the stairs—no good, they were too far.

The dead pit. The walls were steel plating, armored. The dead had tugged the corners free, had tried to tear them off. He could climb them. Use his knife to make handholds further up. Majorca's K-Bar would make a handy off hand climbing tool, as well. He could get to the shattered observation window and then he would be free and clear.

Odds were good, he realized, that he would be leaving Majorca's corpse down here. This fact struck him in the heart with the precision of an ice pick.

He would have to see about coming back down here. Bring Majorca out of this place later. He did not deserve to rot in Hell's antechamber.

First things, of course, first.

Scratching and bumping, almost like knocking. "Who's there?" he almost said, but that would have been crazy. And just what would the answer be? *Lobotomy*, of course. "Lobotomy who?" he would say, and the reply would come, *It don't lobotomy if you come out now or later; sooner or later we'll loboto-you.*

Telling knock-knock jokes to oneself was undoubtedly an early sign of psychosis. Well, if anyone deserved to go crazy, it was Kane. How many friends had he buried? How many friends had he killed? How many walking dead had he insisted lay down for the long deserved rest? That duration of close proximity to death was bound to grow caustic to a man's mind, was bound to cause deterioration.

Of course, if he was infected or sucking Fowler's gas and slowly turning, one of the terminal signs could well be natural mental fail safes shutting down. Then again, he was noticing this process. Didn't that argue for lingering shreds of rationality? The mad, he had once heard, did not know they were crackers, they acted as though their madness was based off incontrovertible proof.

He had long wondered if he was a lunatic drooling on the floor of some psyche ward, hallucinating the end of the world. Wouldn't that be a fitting *Fuck You*?

He opened the door. Three deaders waited outside. They looked startled that the door had actually opened, as though they had not expected their summons to be answered.

His boot shattered the knee of the lead, and he put the other two down with his Desert Eagle. The last one was already trying to crawl forward, but Kane stomped the zombie's face into the floor. He leaned down and fired again. The zombie stopped crawling. Kane moved into the hallway, going quickly but not carelessly. When he heard the sounds of the approaching staggering dead, he abandoned caution and turned his speed up to double quick.

He made it to the Dead Pit as he saw nearing shadow shapes in the spinning emergency lamps. The door could be rigged to close, but it would take time. With the encroaching dead, he worried it was not time he could spare to drag his friend's corpse inside the room. That would leave Majorca's remains out there for the dead to pull apart. A callous man would kick his dead pal aside, and close the door. Kane could be callous when needed, but this was not such a time.

He holstered his weapon and pulled Majorca into a fireman's carry. Dragged him into the Pit. The floor was a bloody mess, but the dead he had left here had not summoned any carrion feeder corpses. That was nice.

The wall panels were torn up, made a seductive set of hand holds leading up the wall. The problem was, there was no way for Kane to know if they would hold his weight. Getting halfway up only to have one of those panels detach from the wall, sending him floorward—possibly to a broken limb or spine—was not an at all attractive idea.

They were coming. The enemy was almost upon him.

The other problem, there would be no climbing while carrying Majorca.

This plan's half-assedness was showing, and Kane muttered invectives. Dangling cables composed a new rub on the already precarious plan—a couple of these could be knotted together to make a nice length. He ripped a set down, found they extended under one of the panels. Dragging this free of the wall revealed a nice surprise—quite the change from the piled on trouble he had been dealing with thus far. One cable gave him sixteen feet of thick, rubber wrapped cord.

A second set was not quite as fruitful—only eight feet. Combined, more than enough.

He wrapped the shorter of the sets around Majorca's shoulders, and around his chest—a standard climber's rig. This he knotted several times, and then D-clipped to the longer of the cables. To make it perfect, he would daub stupid glue on the knots and then blow dry them solid to keep them from coming apart at awkward moments. He had neither the time for this nor the tools. What he had done would have to suffice.

When the first of the dead stormed into the room—a heavy chick, who died in her late teens; the loose skin of her arms swayed like rubbery pendulums with each hurried step, her tattered garments provided little modesty for the rest of her gangrenous flesh—Kane quick drew his pistol like a gunfighter and put her down with a round through the cheek. The back of her head decorated the deader coming behind her. Blinding it for a moment.

Kane glanced up. Leapt. The panel he caught groaned loud as the walking dead by held to the wall. He scampered up, moving to the next, getting his feet out of reach. Half a dozen zombies clawed the walls beneath him. The electrical cord trailed between his belt and Majorca's corpse like an umbilicus.

One of the panels above came free as he reached for it. Fifteen pounds of solid steel slammed into his shoulder and then rode across, sending pain flares burning in his vision. He cursed, and his grip slipped. The struck side went dead, fell to his side to throb a while. He clung by the fingers on one hand, which started to fail when his body whipped around.

Valkyrie Force

The steel panel cut through the air like a fighting kite and cleaved into one of the monsters below, chewing through its face. Kane fought the pain. Swung back around and slammed his shoulder against the wall. He yelped, and shouted, "Work damn you!" and his arm slowly came around. He reached over and clung and tried to keep motionless while he fixed his grip.

The wall plates were biting into his skin. Blood trickled down from his grip, slicking the works. He spat invectives and started up again. Then, he felt the tug from below.

The deaders had found the cord, and one of them figured out they could pull on it and pull on him. It made a kind of sense. These deaders were a hell of a lot smarter than any other deaders he had encountered. Whether it was some kind of natural change or one induced by Fowler's mad experiment did not matter.

They were smart.

The masquerader was smartest of all, but the shamblers were pretty slick too.

A powerful tug stopped all motion. He had to hang on to survive. Hope they gave up.

The steel plate he clung to groaned loudest yet. Began to bend. The tugs from below made the matter no better.

He would have to cut the line.

"I'm sorry, Majorca."

His weak hand dropped to the knife. Drew it out. One thing about the tugging, it made the line taut. Easier to cut a taut line than a loose one.

The black rubber split with an audible sound, and the cut end corkscrewed through the air, landing on the eager tugger's face. The zombie chewed it twice before deciding it was not particularly tasty.

Below, there were almost a dozen moaning undead.

As Kane returned to his climb, only a few of them pounded against the walls or clawed at the panels. The rest tended the waiting meals.

The smacking, feeding sounds, the ripping of clothes and the splatter of flesh and the accompanying wordless complaints as zombies vied for the best sweetbreads brought bile up Kane's throat and shadows into his heart.

Then, he reached the window Majorca had shattered. Inside, he found an observation room with more computers and several cheap office chairs. On the floor, Dr. Brown lay in a bloody heap, her hands clutching gory bits that did not belong to her. She had gone down fighting. A quick check revealed a weak pulse. Shallow breathing. Far gone, but not all the way.

Kane drew his Desert Eagle, did a mental tally of the ammunition, and hoped he would not find a horde of shamblers waiting for him.

In the hallway, lay a collapsed man in a white coat, his round head on the floor to his left. Not Leitch. This man was rounder. Another of the missing persons. In addition to the decapitation, he showed fresh wounds made by a woman's nails—had this been the one to suffer Brown's final wrath?

Possibly. However, Majorca had warned about Leitch. Had the dying man spoken incorrectly? Stress could make the tongue slip, and dying in agony was the ultimate stress imaginable.

Things were no longer quite so clear. So clean.

Kane threw caution to the wind, calling "Leitch!" as he advanced through these unknown hallways.

After two turns, Leitch answered, "How did you get up here?"

"I climbed," Kane said.

"Is everything copacetic?"

"I found a strange setup below," Kane reported. "Demolitions with a computer timer. It's deactivated."

"That sounds like things are copacetic."

"They are."

"Your friend is dead."

Kane said nothing.

"And so is Dr. Brown."

"I'd gathered," Kane said. "Her husband will be devastated."

"She was a smart woman, but stupid in some ways, too. May we leave?"

"Most of the walking dead are trapped below," Kane said. "I can handle any that are up here."

The door opened. Leitch's face appeared. Kane noted the spots around the man's mouth, trace remnants of blood that had been hastily scrubbed away. No mirrors in that room likely. Leitch looked preternaturally calm.

"We have to go," Kane said. "Show me the way out."

"This way," Leitch said.

Five more turns and three zombie kills later, they reached familiar passages. Kane said, "I think I know the way from here."

"Yeah, it's pretty straightforward."

"Fowler abandoned ship pretty fast, didn't he?" Kane asked.

"Yeah," Leitch said. "He knew the end was coming. A smart kind of guy."

"He hasn't been here for a week," Kane said. "Has he?"

Leitch frowned. "I don't know what you're—"

"You've been running his affairs."

"I don't know what you're talking about! I'm a stolen man! I've been held prisoner down here and—"

"Waiting for rescue, sure. But you're no man. Not anymore."

Something dark flashed across Leitch's eyes. It might have been an innocent man's fear, it might have been a guilty thing's disappointment at having been caught. Kane could not say for sure.

"What are you saying, Kane?"

Kane shot Leitch in the face with his last round, hoping he was doing the right thing. Leitch dropped, and Kane holstered his weapon. "As Majorca might have said, 'Adios, el *jeffe*.'"

Kane stepped past the corpse, eyes on the prize: the exit.

Something heavy collided with him, and threw him into the wall. "You know too much!" said Leitch. *Leitch? How?* Kane had shot him in the—

Doesn't matter. Only escape mattered.

The wiry masquerader wrapped his arms around Kane's chest and arms, pinning this last against his side. With incredible strength not evident in the man's frame, Leitch shoved him forward and down. Forcing Kane to his knees.

Kane's gun was empty.

Not that he could do much with it anyway. He had already tried to pop the scientist in the noggin. What the hell *was* he?

"Thought you'd put me down, eh?" Leitch asked. "Your pal tried to do the same, when Brown made her move."

The scientist's arms squeezed tight, cracking Kane's ribs like kindling.

"I'll do you slower than I did either of them. The hunger is so deep, so demanding. Fowler told me not to succumb to it, that to succumb was to start down the path to mindlessness. But with your merry band, I'll take a couple of steps down that ugly road."

The son of a bitch was enjoying this. He delivered pain like it was his vocation, the one task he had squirted into this world to perform.

Kane's hand brushed his belt.

The pommel of his CQC-7B. The knife, he realized, was his one chance.

Leitch's face pressed into his back, he was blind to Kane's specific actions. With some trouble, Kane freed the weapon. Though it drove fresh agony spikes to twist, Kane twisted side-to-side in the man's arms. The illusion of simple struggle was essential to mask his real actions.

Kane's heart pounded machinegun fast. The noise filled his ears with the ceaseless pounding of panic, an engine pushed into the red.

Leitch's curled fingers were locked together like complementary hooks. He squeezed still more, and indescribable pressure built inside Kane's bones. In his chest.

This was the most pain Kane had ever endured. His bowels clenched in the terror that he might squirt his insides into his shorts; his teeth clamped tight to keep them coming out his mouth. He envisioned his own eyes bursting out, on rivers of gore. He imagined his ears spewing like fountains.

Impossible, but terror and reason are ultimately strangers.

Leitch slammed himself flush against Kane's back, now, to increase the power of his assault. A fresh sound joined the rush of his own speedy pulse in his ear. The steady beat of a second heart. Leitch, Kane mused, might be a fiend, but he was not a heartless one after all.

Kane turned his mind to hands. And to the tendons in them.

Unless the dead man was operating from some supernatural reservoir, he had to be guided by the same basic biological truths as other organisms. The dead walked, but even they obeyed the laws that broken bones lacked power, that severed ligaments or tendons made a limb useless.

In the human arm, a complex combination of muscles, nerves and tendons allowed the brain complete control of the wrist and individual digits. Severing the right group, say by sawing through it with a well-used but still quite sharp blade could reduce the effectiveness of the hand.

The most vital of these were the group known as flexor tendons, located along the back of the hand. Well within reach of his knife. Kane reached the CQC-7B's blade up and sawed through the back of Leitch's hand, down to the bone and then slid the blade deeper, as though cutting a wedge from a block of cheese. Leitch made a sound one part surprise, one part outrage, and one part discomfort. Then, the blade struck the wrist and Leitch's offending hand went limp. Leitch did not compensate for this, did not quite know what was happening, and so with a burst of strength, he pulled too hard and ripped his own hand off. Kane fell forward, the pressure in his chest relieved but not removed. He gasped, and turned.

Leitch held up the severed hand to study it with disbelief. The black hole his Desert Eagle had made in the man's face resembled an inscrutable third eye. He gazed from it to Kane, who came forward with his blade. Leitch tried to catch the attack, and Kane finished his riposte, bringing the knife down forward. Into the bastard's still beating heart.

Leitch went pale in an instant. "This can't happen," he said in a nasal whine, and then collapsed like a deflated blow up toy.

Kane pulled his knife free, and sat on his duff. The toxin would take him soon, he knew. He was as good as a deader, now. The dread brought tears to his eyes. He would never see his Valkyrie again.

His earpiece buzzed. Amongst the static, Caul purred his name.

"Get your people out of the building," he said. "There's a hell of a lot of nasty down here. Deaders like you wouldn't believe, explosives, vials of . . . of . . ." He coughed. Blanched at blood taste. "That bastard got me after all. I've been toxined."

She did not offer her condolences. Her response was a surprise: "Don't you give up soldier."

"What? I'm toast. When you see me, put me out of—"

"We got word from the Away Team," Caul said. "What's left of it, anyway . . . They got records on the toxin. There's an antidote, big boy. You'll live to fight another day."

Hope blossomed. Could it be true? Sasha's team had been successful after all?

Kane pushed upright. He fetched Dr. Brown and started toward the door.

"Kane." Fowler's voice came from a speaker on the wall. "I see you, you son of a bitch. *Answer me.*"

So Fowler was still out there, somewhere. He had evaded Sasha and the Away Team. The madman's luck would not last forever.

Kane raised his knife in a mock salute to the ceiling. "Catch you later," he said and stumbled onward. Fowler shouted obscenities and invoked devils, all bearing Kane's name.

He emerged from the madman's scientific womb, hoping the antidote was for real, hoping he would see his girl again, hoping they might put an end to the deader nightmare . . .

End of Valkyrie Force #1

Hungry for more undead ass-kicking action?

Twice Told Tales proudly presents this preview of the exciting second book in the Valkyrie Force series.

Turn the page for:

Damnation Driven

Valkyrie Force

Kane Incarcerated

Isolation did not suit Kane. It gave his mind license to play funny tricks.

He sat in the lifeless isolation room with his back against one blue wall, staring across the slender bed to the other blue wall and wondered if he was going to die and come back, after all. The wall's color was the same shade as a robin's egg – pastel and pale. Supposedly soothing, if you believed the old world's bullshit theories about color therapy and Fung Shue. This choice did nothing to defoliate a grain of the bumper terror crop overgrowing his fertile spirit at wondering if his bloodstream was acting as a delivery system for his own destruction.

His jacket hung over the bed's steel footboard, a frame assembly that resembled a truck's grill more than a bedroom furnishing. In the far corner waited a punching bag; chains secured it to both ceiling and floor. Just in case he felt like burning the calories and working the muscles. Above this, one of two video cameras. They were properly positioned, able to spot him no matter where he might go in the room.

This last element was important if he became . . . unreliable. He would make a particularly nasty unreliable asset, after all.

To behold him was to look backward through time. Kane was a solid looking man, wearing urban camouflage BDU pants, scuffed combat boots and a black tank top. Once upon a time, he might have wielded a broadsword or double bladed axe, which he used to hack and slash his way across a savage wilderness. He certainly looked the sort to rub shoulders with rogues and ne'er-do-wells. Those dazzling blue eyes were the sort to woo a wench at every tavern along a never ending road from rags to royalty. His sandy curls were long enough for said wenches to toy with it, while he tossed back flagon after flagon of mead. Of course, such mythic associations were a ruse. Kane was no reaver, no barbarian, no Hyborean wanderer.

And Kane did not want wenches. He wanted one woman and one woman only: his Valkyrie, *Sasha*. For the moment, he could not have her. The keepers of the keys, the kingdom's masters were holding him away from her with these pastel blue walls.

By his watch, Kane had been in this room for almost three days. The cameras in the corners were trained on him at all times. It was his punishment for walking out of the Boylston Tenement Affair. For being the lone survivor of the sublevel horror show.

Kane wiped a rough palm across his sweaty forehead. The temperatures in this space were unbearable. Just short of a swelter. The sorts of temps he had endured in godforsaken jungles in geographic locations few Americans could spell or correctly identify on a map. Places a covert American presence was needed to make the world safe. Now, America didn't matter anymore. Hadn't for over a decade. It was a place on an old, old map. It was an idea that had snuffed out.

Still, the memories remained.

The pleasant ones: Sasha's lovely body. Her gorgeous curves. The ways they moved and responded to his touch. She was the one bright light he had encountered since the dead rose from the grave and the world went to shit. She was a pillar of stability in a world gone insane. A world born in those other memories, the haunting ones. The violent ones.

In this blue, blue room, he often thought about those godforsaken places he had traveled and the things he had done there. Usually killing or arranging situations and explosives to perform killing. The government he swore eternal faith to called these black bag jobs. He called them work.

Kane had been born a killer, reared as a killer, and . . . But he would not think about the man who had first made him kill.

He would not think about his father. Would not give that old bastard's shade the satisfaction.

A slat near the door's lower edge opened. A tray moved in, shoved across the floor by a unseen broomstick operator. The prisoner's evening meal: chicken fried steak, an onion and pork kebob, a bowl of kale and corn, and a sweet potato. Steel utensils instead of plastic. He took this to be a good sign. Also, a bottle of water and a can of beer. A piece of best-forgotten history, this last: A dented can of Proud to be Your Domestic Swills that was little different from water.

The slat shut before he could thank his provider or ask how much longer he was to remain in here. How much longer his keepers were going to incarcerate him.

No matter. They would not have answered.

The meal sucked, but he shoveled it into his mouth through a regular rotation of the utensils. Eating rats in South American and southeast Asian hell holes had taught him how to make the plate to mouth windmill motion work. He chewed for proteins, carbohydrates, vitamins and minerals and not for subtle luxuries like flavor. A long enough time in the jungle took away the needs for such niceties. That was isolation of a different sort.

The government referred to it as MIA. He considered it LB, Left Behind.

When he was done eating, he washed it down with half the water. Popped the tab on the beer. This, he did pause to savor. First beer of the day was worth enjoying, even if it was domestic. The pencil pushers operating this little isolation tank waited to open the bars until after six o'clock. But why?

Once the dead got up and started walking around, why should a bar close at all?

Kane supposed the penny pushers and the bean counters would always be with the world. So long as three human beings existed, one of them would possess, one of them would want and the third would seek to quantify, qualify and entangle the whole act of desire/possession with bureaucratic bullshit.

Domestic beer had never been all that tasty. It had to do with heat applied during the fermentation, which speed up the reaction at the cost of flavor. He recalled the ads for the chugging can, designed to be opened and consumed in no time flat. That way, there was no danger of getting turned off by flavor. There was only the buzz. Age did nothing for this one. It tasted little better than foamy water.

Damn, America was in one hell of a bind before the end came for it. The world, he supposed, was in the same damned bind. The dead rising was just a way to start over.

With a grimace, he realized: *This room temperature swill cannot be savored, after all.* Not like the stuff Majorca had made.

Majorca. His brother in arms, now gone. Dead because Kane had made one big whopping mistake.

If you ruminate on the folks you kill, his mind twisted his old man's words, *all is lost.*

He studied the can instead, seeing the friendly logo, some long dead and probably devoured marketing exec's design ideas to communicate the unspoken promise that this beer was a boon companion, a trusted friend, a pal who would never judge, never blame and never leave. *Waste not, want not.* He drained the last of the can's contents in two mouthfuls. Afterward, Kane crushed the can and tossed it on the tray.

Before unleashing a throaty belch, he said, "Banzai, motherfuckers," and smiled to himself. Different memory, that. Captain Cornhole in the back of a slick, tossing belches and beer cans past the huey's M-60 mount. He had been a big man with a surprisingly small voice. The Congo's emerald hell swallowed each offering without comment. Of course, it would claim its real tribute later. The Captain never humped out of that bush . . .

Before the world ended, how many people did I know who stuck around longer than a few years? Not many. He could count them on one hand. The Captain had been one. He was the man who took the trash Kane had been and molded him into a warrior. Other than him? No one, really . . .

His world granted new perspective, Kane slid the tray to the door hatch with a boot tip.

He caught a whiff of himself. Not terrible, yet. He did not smell like he was rotting. He just smelled sweaty.

It had been nine meals since he'd showered – figure three days. The grime was crusting. The air conditioning made it far more luxurious than squatting for three days in some central American jungle, squatting in some desert trawler's gunner's turret while the night turned downright frigid and icicles threatened to descend from your nutsack, or humping through a southeast Asian hell with a twenty-five pound pack on your back and a nine pound weapon in your arms.

Time to get a good sweat on. He shucked his BDUs and boots, padded around in shorts and tank. He hit floor to pound out one hundred pushups followed by one hundred crunches. Then he was up and dancing with the bag, landing a few powerful haymakers and several light but fast jabs. He leaned on the bag, while the sweat rolled. While the breath caught in his lungs or clawed for position in his throat. The workout burn felt good. Muscles screaming for more use, more punishment. He returned to the bag for a little Muay Thai refreshers, following sets of spinning, jumping and double leg kick techniques with sets of open hand, closed hand and pressure-point hand strikes.

By the time he was done, the black tank clung to his back and chest, like an MMA opponent begging for mercy. His neck, pits and crotch were soaked. A fire roared through his muscles and mind, scouring away the dregs of nostalgic nonsense, past pains and current drear.

If he was going to die from the Boylston snafu, it would have happened already, right?

Three days was more than enough time for him to become unreliable. To be *compromised*. Surely, he would have succumbed and then reanimated by now?

He dropped back onto his place on the floor, sat with his back to the wall and waited for his release.

It did not come for two more days.

When the door's lock opened with a loud, grating clack, on the other side stood dowdy city manager Dwight Slown along with two beefy men toting shotguns. "The Mayor," Slown said, "wants to speak with you

Kane." His grin held a threat, but as he observed Kane's nearly naked body, that threat lightened. Something sinister remained, but a nervous wistfulness tugged at his features.

"Oh, does he, now?" Kane pushed himself upright at his own speed, taking this moment to assert his will. To sow a little anarchy. He held his hands to either side, showing off his sweat drenched body. Oh yeah, he thought, Slown was eyeing him up and down as though he was cut from marble and stuck in a museum. "As you can see, I'm already dressed for the occasion."

"Why don't you prepare first?" Slown asked.

"Why don't I?"

To the shotgun men, Slown said, "Bathe him."

He retrieved his jacket and clothes. Slown held out a brown paper grocery sack. On the side, the logo for the long lost Trader Joe's in Shrewsbury, across Lake Quinsigamond. "In here, Kane."

"I don't think I'll fit."

Slown's face pinched with impatience. "Your clothes, Kane." Before he even finished speaking, Kane had stuffed his garments in the offered sack. "Good boy, Kane."

"Good boy, Moneypenny," Kane said.

"That's not my name," Slown said. "I'm—"

"You're Dwight Slown," Kane interrupted. "I was attempting to make a funny." Slown's surprise was comic. Kane wondered: *Doesn't anyone remember your name, Mister Slown?* To the shotgun toting toughs, he said, "Lead on, boys."

Chapter One: Free To Die

Naked, mighty Kane stood with his back to a white tiled wall while the two guards turned a fire hose on him. The blast of water made him want to curl up, to protect his vital parts. Slown watched the whole affair with a sadist's eagerness.

The harsh spray ran all along his body, pounding him like a hundred icy, steel toed combat boot kicks per second. This was an echo of the treatment he had gotten while spending three months in a Cambodian prison pit, after an operation took a turn for the rotten.

He stood as long as he could, cursing the bastards for this treatment. "I'm not the enemy," he screamed. "I'm not the fucking enemy." They did not listen. Instead, they played their games, leering until the water finally stopped.

Slown asked, "Were you ever in the Navy, Kane?"

"No."

"But I suppose you know about Navy showers?" Slown tossed him a cake of soap. "Tick-tock, hero. Tick-tock."

Kane snarled and grabbed the cake. Started rubbing his numb, frigid flesh as quickly as he could.

A Navy shower, Slown had said. Kane was familiar with the idea. Although it seemed contradictory: when the military's big battleships were on duty, water was a valuable commodity, a metered resource. Sure, water was everywhere, but as the old saying went there was neither a drop to drink nor to bathe in. Salt water left a body feeling bloated, unclean. That was all there was to find on the big wet of the Atlantic, Pacific or Indian oceans. Fresh water was necessary for both consumption and cleanliness. With the massive numbers of crewmen aboard the ship, recycling cleaning water was mandatory. However, that was not enough to guarantee enough H2O for everyone. An additional conservation step was taken: Navy regs instituted mandatory time limits for showering: the water was turned on for thirty seconds to allow the seaman to get his entire body wet, followed by one waterless minute for soap and shampoo, concluding with another thirty seconds of water to rinse all the suds off.

The hose had been on longer than thirty seconds. The pounding pressure had felt like an eternity, but Kane's internal chronometer told him those goons had sprayed him down for not quite three actual minutes.

"There's no reason for this," Kane said. "We're on the same—" *Side*, he did not get to finish saying. And *The living*, he never got to explain which side he meant.

Slown said, "Time," and the hose turned back on. He added, "You missed behind your ears," and mimed daintily scrubbing.

Fury rose in Kane, its heat battling the frigid blast. The big man had spoken true: There was no reason for this. No rational explanation. Plenty of irrational ones, though.

Two kinds of men were drawn to power. The first type sought to use the position to accomplish good deeds. These were your crusaders and general good folks. The second category used their attained positions to satisfy their own ambitions. These were your pissants seeking puissance, the jackasses heady with revenge fantasies that included such disparate fiends as apathetic dictators, petty tyrants and corrupt cops using the authority to bash a few heads solely for the reason that the bashers needed targets. The second category had outnumbered the first when the world was a zombie free shithole. After that world ended, after the veneer of civility had been clawed away by the living dead's hands, the second category got all the more opportunities to satisfy their lust, greed and need.

Slown was a case in point.

When the water sprayed over his legs and groin, Kane hit the floor. Curled into a ball. The water roared over him a little longer, and then mercifully shut off.

After two dozen heartbeats of hearing the hose still roaring in his head, Kane realized Slown was talking: "Are you ready to behave, tough guy?"

Never, Kane thought, but he said, "Yes," filling it with as much humility as possible. Let that Slown bastard decide Kane was broken. Let him gloat over his minor victory. Kane would wait for his opportunity, and—

"Missed a spot," Slown said. The hose came back on, and cleaned the suds from Kane's hair. Try to cow him as it might, it left the dark thoughts blossoming like sick roses inside his skull.

\#

The men gave him a towel when they were done. Watched him dry off. Kane said nothing, but performed his task with quick, thorough practice. He dressed with the same efficiency. Slown led the way from the prison to the transport in the street outside, he sat across from Kane wearing a proud smirk during the five minute drive.

Kane glanced at the dim monitors as they rode, getting a limited view of the outside world. Sodium arc lamps gave the gray buildings a cadaverous quality. They rode past the Brazilian section, seeing tenements stuffed to bursting with the "undesirables." Before Ruin had settled, Massachusetts had one of the highest populations of Brazillian immigrants in the country. They had been urged into ghettos, and the thread of subtle racism continued to bind them there. These folks clustered like sardines into lousy living conditions. As night settled over the city, they gathered in yards, around barrels and grills alive with fire, or perched atop balconies and porch roofs, playing guitars and giving festivity where none could otherwise be found. "What are they celebrating?" Slown wondered, shaking his head. "Lazy bastards are always *celebrating* . . . But what? There's nothing *to* celebrate."

Kane wondered: *What about life? Isn't that enough?* "What would you prefer they do?"

"They should be indoors," Slown grumbled. "Sleeping. Resting for tomorrow's work day."

"Aren't you afraid?" Kane asked.

"Afraid of what?"

"That when they stop celebrating," Kane said, "and take a look at how they are living, then they might get disgruntled. Dissatisfied."

"Dissatisfaction makes a man work harder," Slown said, and Kane realized he had no understanding about notions such as privilege or powder kegs.

The transport lumbered on.

When they arrived outside City Hall, Slown led the way up the steps, once again puffed like a proud bird.

When they got to the Mayor's office, Slown announced Kane with the cordial solemnness due a visiting dignitary, and then stepped aside. The room was tastefully decorated with brown leather and bookshelves, almost everything spoke of stolid reverence for the United State of America that was, and the long history of leadership and vision that dead nation had espoused.

The man standing behind the massive, dark stained wooden desk was a wiry fellow, physically small. Five foot five at most, but built powerfully. He gazed out the window overlooking the city. His city. When he turned to greet his guest, Kane found the Mayor to be a perfect specimen of the fighting Irish gangster stock that populated pre-apocalypse south Boston—gaunt and red haired, with a fiery goatee and brilliant blue eyes. Everything about him betrayed careful attention to grooming, from his trim hair to the recently pressed shirt, to the crease along his slacks, to the shine on his shoes. The eyes, however, gave away the reptilian soul inhabiting the man, there was nothing warm or remotely human within.

"Kane," he said and offered a hand. His lips raised in a tight grimace when Kane did not immediately accept it. With a twist of the wrist, the offered greeting shifted to indicate a nearby chair. Dark stained wood, blood red cushion. Great shape for having survived Armageddon. "Won't you have a seat?"

"I prefer to stand," Kane said.

At one of the Mayor's steely glances, Slown said, "Sit Kane." A shotgun toting thug kicked Kane behind the knee, sending the big man to a crouch. Slown shoved the chair over.

"You misunderstand our relationship," the Mayor said. "I am the caretaker of an entire city."

"A city my people saved from destruction," Kane snapped. He groaned as he pulled himself into the chair. "That deserves a little recognition. Hell, even a 'Thank you.' I'm not the enemy here."

"Aren't you?" the Mayor said. "The problem with your perspective, Kane is this: you think there is only one truth. In fact, there are many forms of truth. There is the truth of the story you have told about what you found under a tenement in the heart of our city. A finding and an activity, which I heartily thank you for handling with timeliness and finality. A mess our flame units had less trouble eradicating all traces of, once they received your report. That is the truth you should be congratulated for, and which, here in this office, I can. You did well. However . . ."

Kane's blood froze in his veins. This story had a familiar opening, something he had heard about many times when he was a junior operative in the bad old days during the human dominance of this planet.

"However, there is also the truth as the people know it. That a rogue agent scheduled a clear and sweep operation in a downtown tenement in order to loot personal effects from the underprivileged persons living in said building."

"You sold me out like that?"

"Would you rather have me tell people your truth?"

Kane considered this. If people knew that enemy agents had taken over an old underground black ops facility under Protective Services' very noses, they would lose what little faith they possessed in the system. Faith and trust were even more vital than ever, in this cowardly new world of the walking dead.

"I see you agree with me." The Mayor chuckled. "Whether or not you want to verbally admit to it does not matter. It is the story that needed to be shared."

Kane wondered about the missing persons he had found down there. The vanished scientists. It would be easy to keep them on the books as missing, he supposed. Their families and friends be damned: this was a tough old world all over. And what of the biochemist Trini Brown who had made it out alive though comatose? Kane had heard nothing of her fate.

The Mayor continued: "The city council understands this truth, and they have been calling for the rogue agent's head. We will supply them with one. Whether or not that head belongs to you is a matter for consideration, however."

"I'm listening."

"We agree that this Dr. Darren Fowler person is a menace. A threat to life, liberty and the Worcester way."

"You could say that."

"We want him removed. But we want it done in a way that will not worry our citizens."

"Or," Slown added, reminding Kane that he was still present, "the city council."

"Right," the Mayor said. "Especially not them."

"Ah," Kane said. He knew the black ops work offer would be coming up next. When the world had ended, he had expected this kind of behind the scenes bullshit to end. He had almost come to believe that *In the Public's Best Interest* was a phrase that would forever be relegated to the history books. Or if not forever, then it would not resurface until well after some of kind reconstruction.

"Since the Ruin," the Mayor said, "it has become a survival skill to keep an eye on cost-benefit ratios."

"Counting beans," Kane said, "to make sure the beans don't unexpectedly run out."

"We don't want to kick anyone out of our city. Warm bodies are important for many, many reasons. However, we cannot give the warm bodies we *have* any reason to doubt our competence. We do not need exoduses. We certainly do not need *revolts*."

"So, you want someone who can kick ass for you, without calling attention to his activities. You want someone who knows the difference between true stories and *necessary* ones."

The Mayor's face lit up with calculated cues for empathy his eyes did not show. "We want someone versed in those things most of all."

"Someone like you, Kane," Slown added.

"Someone like me."

The Mayor sat down behind his desk. From a drawer he produced a page and slid it across the desk. "Recognized this, Kane?"

Kane scanned the paper. It was a proposal he had made almost six months ago. "The Valkyrie Force," he read. "A mobile solution to an ever changing problem." Sasha's pal Wheelz had come up with the action item list for dealing with the last threat to the city, he had named the operation after her call sign. "It got shit canned, if I recall."

"It did," the Mayor said. "It got rejected because the City Council rightly read it as an incredible tax on resources for an undefined return."

"Also," Slown added, "it was tied to a renegade. You."

"Beans have to be cooked to make them edible," Kane said. "A filled granary's stores will rot, if they aren't used. You have to invest in a safe future by—"

"Oh, you're preaching to the choir on this one," the Mayor said. "The problem is you tried to use official channels. If you had put this before me and made the compelling case you just did, I would have agreed whole heartedly."

"Too late now," Kane said.

"Is it?" asked Slown.

Kane said, "The Council—"

"I have some discretionary powers," the Mayor said. "They allow me to ensure our safety. To equip the Protective Services and whatnot . . ."

"You want to activate my Valkyrie Force idea?"

"I want to activate," the Mayor repeated, "the Valkyrie Force idea. With two caveats."

Here it comes. The hook was out. All that remained were the two acts of lining and sinking. "And those are."

The Mayor smiled, "Someone needs to be held accountable. True leaders stand behind every decision and action taken by their team."

He sent the paper back across the desk. "You want me to be the public face." It was a bad choice of words, and he knew it.

"I want you to be one hundred percent accountable for every action taken by your team."

The Mayor had already decided this was going to happen, Kane realized. There was no opportunity to say no. Of course, Kane was never a fan of anyone's assumption that he would tow the party line. The bad old days were dead and gone. It was a new world.

"As such," the Mayor said, "once this Fowler character is taken care of, you will stand trial before the Council and you will take whatever punishment they mete out. I will be your silent provider, your guardian angel until that time. Once Fowler is dispatched . . ."

"Then it would be in my best interest to clear out of Worcester," Kane said, "and never return. That about it?"

"I would never encourage fugitives to run from justice," the Mayor said, but the underlying message was there. *Go and live, stay and suffer.*

Kane asked, "And the second caveat?"

"I will not be compromised," the Mayor said. "You do not tell a soul, either living or dead, about this arrangement. Not your girl, not your priest, not your dear sainted mother. Not one damned person." A single, slender finger rose to emphasize the point. "If you do, then you're done."

"I will have to tell them something," Kane said. "My people, I mean."

"We have a story for you," Slown said. "A cover, if you will. Something you can sink your teeth into."

"I'll leave it to Slown to tell you the details. Now, as you have no more questions, I'll kindly ask—"

"What's in this for me?"

"Excuse me?"

Slown said, "Shut your trap, Kane."

Kane ignored the sycophant. "Since I did the last thing you wanted, I've been stuck in solitary confinement, had my reputation smeared all to Hell, and been given the choice between eventual banishment, imprisonment or a death sentence. I don't see why I should help you do any damned thing." His voice was little louder than a snake's hiss. "I'm free to die on my own terms, why should I take yours?"

"You're thinking too much about yourself," the Mayor said. "Think about this, Kane: I'm not offering you a shit deal for your future. We already live in a shit world. The future for everyone still walking is terminally grim on the best day. I'm offering you one thing you want more dearly than anything else."

"And what's that?"

"Dr. Fowler's head," the Mayor said. "I'm giving you the resources and the opportunity to hunt him down and kill him like the mad dog he is."

Kane considered this. And then he wondered if he really wanted to live in Worcester at all. The world was an ugly place, sure, rife with disease, treachery and the walking dead. Whoville was a microcosm of corruption and despair, though. It probably did not seem that way for the folks who lived there—the folks living on the other side of the curtain, that was. Those who kept their heads down probably thought it was good to have a council and mayor they could trust to make the hard choices. The great democracy had degenerated into serfs and royalty.

"I'll take your resources," Kane said. "And your opportunity."

"Excellent. We knew you weren't a fool. Not our Valkyrie Force Commandant." The Mayor stood once more, and the dusk colored his thin face with red death. He extended his hand. "Are you my man, Kane?"

Kane considered the offered hand. His eyes flashed up to meet the Mayor's. "I'm nobody's bitch."

"You may have believed so, before," the Mayor said, his reptilian eyes flashing with an alien sensation that might have been perceived as humor. "Now, however, you most certainly are. And you are mine."

Kane stood, feeling the tension in the shotgun men behind him. In the periphery, he caught a glance of Slown tensing as well. "Then I suppose I'm your man," Kane said. His hand enveloped the Mayor's, "for as long as it takes to deliver Fowler's head."

"Glad to hear it," the Mayor said. He grimaced when Kane amped up the strength in his hand, but he refused to cry out or whimper. The Mayor had stones, all right.

Valkyrie Force

"And when this is all over," Kane said, "when the world is a better place, I'll be visiting you for another one of these uplifting chats." Kane released the man before his thugs intervened.

"I look forward to it," the Mayor said, shaking feeling back into his numb digits. "Get him on his damned way."

Slown and the goons led him from the room. Kane walked with head held high.

Chapter Two: Bleed Out

They stopped off in the city's motor pool. The Umass Medical School's four story parking structure that stood near Plantation Street no longer serviced grad students, medical students, doctors or nurses, it now held light armor and cavalry vehicles on the first three floors. The fourth held a pair of Apache attack choppers and a Quonset. Kane got his briefing in the Quonset, amongst the choppers' repair kits and spare parts. The two shotgun men posed near the door, rifles slung and hands upon their pistols.

When the little frog of a toady told him the cover story, Kane did not bother holding his laughter. He guffawed in the man's face. "That's the stupidest idea I have ever heard, Slown." *If not the most foolish, then certainly in the top five.*

Even with Kane sitting in an uncomfortable wooden chair, with the toady standing over him, the guy was still as small as a worm. It was all presence and character, Kane supposed. This guy was stunted on all fronts.

Valkyrie Force

Slown's features turned down into a surprisingly believable approximation of an anthropomorphic stoat's disapproval. He said, "That's the story we will be supporting, Kane. And you will not be leaving this room until you can spit it back to me verbatim. Do you under—?"

"The Valkyrie Force," Kane recited, "is a specially selected team of agents from Protective Services, charged with the ultimate defense of the fortified city of Worcester. We are men and women elected to the position for our dedication and demonstrated elite techniques. Our authority reaches not only wall to wall, but to the surrounding terrain as well." Kane cocked an eyebrow. "It's a bunch of words that say absolutely nothing. Why not just call us the Avengers and be done with it?"

"The Avengers?" Slown's forehead crinkled with uncertainty. "But you're the *Valkyrie Force*. That other name is an unfamiliar—"

"Sorry for the confusion," Kane said. "Tell me about our resources."

"I'm not convinced you are as on board as the Mayor believes. Recite the protocol, again."

"Are you kidding me?"

"Are you looking for another shower?" Slown asked. "One can be arranged." One of the goons chuckled at this. The height of bullshit comedy.

Kane recited the cover story, again. More slowly, this time. He kept his humor out of it. Slown followed along, mouthing the words Kane spoke while bobbing his head as though participating in a octogenarian's rock concert version. When he was done, the big man sat in silence while Slown considered the words.

"Satisfactory," Slown said.

"Sir," Kane said, "thank you, sir."

Slown puffed at the verbal respect. "I bet you were a good soldier, once."

Kane said nothing because there was nothing to say.

"We have decided you will need a squad of six persons. Yourself as leader. A driver, a mechanic, a medic, a gunner and a communications person."

"I will actually need a seventh member," Kane said, adding "sir" like the afterthought it was.

"Oh?"

"Yes. An Intelligence officer."

"That makes sense."

Kane refrained from asking if Slown wanted to add a Loyalty or Propaganda officer. "May I pick my personnel?"

"We have some options for you, but yes."

Kane already knew who he wanted, but he would indulge Slown's puffed up pride and take a look at the options. "And my team's resources?"

"They will vary from operation to operation," Slown said. It was the universal sign of you'll get what we want you to have when we want you to have it. "You will have an LAV-25A2 to start with. It's an amphibious vehicle, used—"

"Used by the USMC until the Marine Personnel Carrier replaced them," Kane said. He recalled the eight wheeled vehicles as low riding and hella loud. Three man crew, plus room for six more. They came in numerous options, including tank busters or mortar equipped. He was likely to get the typical stripped down model, with a M242 "Bushmaster" 24mm cannon and mounts for machineguns and grenade launchers. He asked, "How about firepower?"

"Small arms for your unit and mounted guns."

"Explosives?"

Slown cocked an eyebrow. "Availability will vary."

"I see. What can we count on when we're on LRRP? Forget the variability. What will always be in our kits?"

"For now? Base survival rations and camping equipment. You will be given enough gas to reach your destination and return, but not much more than that."

"Keeping the leash tight, huh?"

Slown nodded. "For now. As you show how loyal you are, we will give you more autonomy."

"Do we know where Fowler is, today?"

"Not exactly," Slown said, "but we've got some leads."

"Leads?"

"First, we want to try you out on a . . . a low scale operation."

Kane did not bother telling Slown that this was a clear violation of the agreement he had made with the Mayor. Such a protest would have done two things: *no* and *good*. "And that would be?"

"While your woman was getting most of her team killed on her fool's errand earlier this week," Slown said, practically snarling, "she managed to come across enough useful intelligence to keep her out of quarantine."

"It saved my life," he said. Wherever Sasha had been, she had learned the antidote to the death toxin Fowler had secreted under the city. "Her team died?"

"Most of them," Slown said. "If she hadn't broadcast her information on Worcester's open signal, we would've had her in a cell next to yours." He sounded damned disappointed Sasha had escaped such a fate.

"And are we tracking down more antidote or something?"

"No," Slown said. "She identified a series of compounds across the countryside. Each connected via some kind of secret communications lines. She hit one, left it leaderless. The forces stationed there detonated the place, erasing any sign of life."

"You want us to visit another," Kane said, "and see what we can find?"

"And report back to us," Slown said. "If the bad Doctor is there, you will kill him, of course."

Kane grunted.

"But seeking him out is not the first priority. Understanding their defenses is. Their comm lines, if possible. If we can intercept their messages, then we will be in a better place to guarantee our safety."

Rationales were for academics. Fowler was a lunatic and the enemy, that was the only rationale Kane needed. If this broken world was to move forward with its reconstruction, the lunatics and enemies would have to be dealt with. Harshly. Permanently. Still, Kane grunted again, to make Slown feel better. Vital.

"Do you understand?" Slown asked. "Give me full verbal verification."

"I understand," Kane said, while he wondered about the best ways to kill this toad of a man. He would not do so immediately, of course. Slown would have to live for a while. But eventually . . . *Soon*. The bastard would get his ticket punched, and Kane longed to be there. The toad was just as rotten to the core as Fowler, though he hid it beneath a veneer of lapdog civility.

Of course, should Kane start with Slown, he might have to keep going. Purge Worcester of the selfish, greedy, bestial bastards abusing their positions of power.

Sometimes, though, such people were necessary. Kane knew they were. The Mayor, for example, was not above being cruel. The difference between him and this lackey, this Slown, was pretty obvious: the Mayor had his fingers on the bigger picture's pulse; his cruelty served the Greater Good. This little bastard was mean simply because he could be, and the bitch of it all was this: Slown probably did not know he was a bully or a prick. He probably thought he was the same as his boss.

"And what's next?" Kane asked.

"Next," Slown said, "you recite the purpose again."

Kane rattled it off like his name, rank and serial number. The situation for both sets of information was pretty much the same: he was a prisoner looking for release.

"And again," Slown said.

Kane recited it again, while thinking about wrapping his hands around Slown's neck and squeezing. Watching the man's eyes bulge as he gasped for air. He fantasized about the surprise the man would go through.

"Now, you get to pick your team."

"Actually, let's hit the Canteen. I want to see Sasha first."

"Your woman? There's no time—"

"She's going to be my Intelligence officer, Slown. That means there's time."

"But our prepared options! We determined likely candidates—"

"I've decided on that role," he said. "Hell, I *created* it. There were no options for that particular job, remember?"

Slown pouted, outsmarted and hating the shameful feelings this brought him. In the back of all this, he was plotting, but Kane thought: *Damn your plots, Slown.*

"After I give her the good news," Kane said, "then we will pick the team and get along on our merry damned way to certain death. That good enough for you? Sir?"

#

The Umassmed depot and supply station straddled Plantation Street. Perched along the north side of Route 9, it offered a beautiful view of tranquil Lake Quinsigamond as well as the ruins of old Shrewsbury beyond. The building was a milestone for the pre-Ruin city, a world class medical school with hundreds of millions of dollars in government funding coming in every year. After the rise of the dead and subsequent fall of mankind, it remained a vital medical post, as well as a military one.

Protective services took over a large piece of the main campus to use as a supply center. Across Plantation Street, the men could use the hilly section that had once housed Biotech industry and external Umass buildings to run drills.

Kane had to admit It was gruesome but efficient to combine the intensive care hospital with a high grade munitions facility. Men could respond to post-life medical emergencies double quick, and way the hell over on the east end of the city as it was, the hospital could be easily blown to bits if something got too far out of control.

That last part was speculation, of course. No one wanted to admit whether they had lined the lower floors with enough explosives to level the building completely. Spoken or not, Kane would have initiated that tactic. And added incendiaries to make sure nothing walked out of the rubble.

Not a block down the 9 waited the north end of Shrewsbury Street. Before the Ruin, this was Worcester's hot street. Expensive restaurants and bars, which would get community choked past reason on weekend nights, and hum with activity through the week days. It retained some of that air, serving as the go-to strip for both med center and protective service folks.

No car needed, you could walk.

Kane opted to walk, and Slown, still rubbing at his sore pride, decided to walk with him. He really should have ridden.

Valkyrie Force

The fastest way to Shrewsbury Street by foot was to cut across Plantation Street and walk through the training woods. A fifteen minute walk past the Beechwood Hotel's remnants and in sighting distance of the old Abbot Biotechnology building would take pedestrians to the far sidewalk and the fading crosswalk.

Though shadowed, Kane knew the oaks and maples were burning with autumn colors. The air was rich with the scent of autumn. Crisp breezes carried the distant aroma of burning leaves and the last grilling bouts of the season. Kane's steady pace kicked up hundreds of crunches from old leaves, curled like clutching fingers.

Slown was not in a shape conducive to walking for long. He slumped against a tree, calling for everyone to stop with him by demanding, "Do you have to go so fast, Kane?"

Kane paused, allowing the human balloon to catch his breath. His two aids paused with weapons slung, lighting up cigarettes. They chattered amiably, and Kane realized this was the first time they had acted at all human.

"How long you two been in Protective?" Kane asked.

"Seven months," the first said. He had a square jaw, wire rimmed glasses and massive pectorals. His name tag identified him Walkowitz.

"Almost a year," his partner said, stand offish. This was a round bellied specimen of Black Irish. McDonald, his name tag identified him. He had been the shower hose's operator. Walkowitz had been a gleeful assistant.

McDonald held out the pack to Kane, who waved *thanks but no thanks*. The Irishman said, "You know you're going to die, right? Cigarettes might speed that up, but not a whole hell of a lot."

"Not feeling one, just now," Kane said.

"I don't understand why we're walking at all," Slown complained, and all eyes returned to him.

The man really wants attention, Kane thought, and that was when the dead girl came around the tree Slown leaned against, all hunger in her large eyes and clutching hands.

She had been maybe ten when she passed, and pretty. A slip of a Caucasian with dark hair and green eyes. These elements were still evident in her features. Time, however, had not been good to this little girl. She still wore a pretty lemon yellow dress with crinoline, though these things were ruined by time and wear. She wore a single Mary Jane shoe, the sock bunched around her ankle. Her other foot was bare and home to several gaping wounds. Her death had not been a quiet one; the waxy, yellow complexion bespoke a wasting sickness of some kind. The puffiness around her eyes writhed with carrion. From the ragged holes in her cheek, throat and arms, her death had not been a quiet one. Not shamblers, these marks looked like the work of hungry wildlife—rats or cats. Small dogs, maybe.

She moved with speed and viciousness. The insatiable hunger motivated her to be a good little consumer. A land shark.

She latched onto Slown's arm. Kane realized the toady was frozen with fright. His men were foolishly unslinging their shotguns—blasts at this range would dispatch both the girl and the toady. If Kane did nothing, Slown would be dead in seconds.

But he could not stand by. As the girl dragged her mouth to Slown's fleshy arm, the big man raced forward. Fungus had colored her incisors a nasty algae green. He slammed a fist into her face, and sent her head back and to the side. She chomped on air.

McDonald's shotgun came to bear on all three of them, and Kane lashed out with a boot. He kicked the rifle up, and the blast killed

Valkyrie Force

October colored leaves and tree limbs. Debris fell around the combatants like confetti.

Kane clapped the little girl's head between his hands and gave it a savage twist. Her spine snapped, and her body lost its rigidity like a puppet without guidelines. Her jaws still clapped open shut open shut, but no motivators remained.

Then, Sloan let out a second screech.

The little girl, Kane discovered, had not been alone. A little boy— maybe an older brother, similar hair and eyes, similar state of body damage and decay, perhaps three years older when he croaked—had appeared on the other side of the tree. He had Slown in a death grip and there was nothing Kane could do.

Slown finally proved himself able. Showed the survival skills that had seen him through the Ruin's special rings of hell. The dead boy was almost five feet tall. A solid, chubby cheeked kid who had lost his guts through a ragged rend in his belly. Slown hefted the boy like a caber and tossed him aside, sparing himself.

The dead child flipped through the air, and Kane ducked to avoid this unintentional flying tackle. The boy flew past. Right into McDonald's arms. The dead boy was not picky. He scampered to McDonald's exposed throat and gnawed. The protection services man dropped to his ass, screaming and slapping. Not thinking, his pal Walkowitz tried to save McDonald with a shotgun blast. The dead boy moved at the wrong time, however.

The shotgun roared, ripping a fresh hole through the kid's back and into McDonald's chest. The air clouded with freshly released blackflies, mold spores and screams. McDonald's gore splatted the trunk, the boy, the earth and Kane.

While Walkowitz cocked a fresh shell into the chamber, Kane grabbed McDonald's weapon by the barrel and swung it like a club. The butt smacked the boy in the side and sent him in a line drive away. Past the tree he had come around. By the time he got to his feet, Kane had a proper grip on his weapon. He and Walkowitz blew the dead boy to hell.

McDonald groaned. Moaned. Pleaded, using half words.

"Help him," Slown said. "Help him."

Kane snapped, "Help who?"

Slown waved toward the bleeding soldier like he was shooing something away. "Help *him*."

You don't even know his name, Kane realized. "He's bit and blasted. He's going to die."

"Then shoot him!" Slown demanded, panic giving his words extra doses of urgency. "Shoot him in the goddamn head!"

When Walkowitz grudgingly raised his rifle, Kane used McDonald's barrel to move that weapon away. "No, Slown. You do it."

"Me?" His head dragged side-to-side in the universal signal of *no fucking way.*

"Yes," Kane said. He held McDonald's weapon out for the toady to take. "This is your fault."

"I didn't put those dead kids out there!"

"No, but you reacted without thinking," Kane said stoically. "You killed this man to save your skin. You are responsible for finishing his passage. Put him down."

"I don't," Slown said, "I don't even know how to load—"

Kane racked a fresh cartridge into the shotgun's chamber. "Push the barrel to his forehead. Squeeze the trigger. It's easy to make another man do it. It's not so easy to do it yourself."

Slown paled, wiping excess saliva from his mouth. He looked ready to vomit within the next few seconds.

If not before the kill, Kane wagered, *then certainly after*. With sudden amazed wonder, he asked "Haven't you dispatched the dying before?"

The toady shook his head in an almost imperceptible negation.

Slown had never killed? That was one cherry Kane did not know could still exist in this Ruined world. Except amongst newborns, maybe. "Well, now you will."

"No," Slown said, sounding like a petulant child. *I don't want to!*

Kane shoved the weapon into Slown's arms. He caught it reflexively. Kane nudged the barrel down to McDonald's head. "All set here."

McDonald stared past the barrel, into Kane him with both hatred and misery.

"Jesus, man," Walkowitz said. "Don't. Not like. Not like this."

"Turn away if you must," Kane said. He would not. Someone needed to bear witness, and Slown was not the man to both perform as pity executioner *and* witness. "Ready, Slown? Then squeeze."

Slown blubbered. "I can't. I *can't*." But he did. The shotgun roared. McDonald's face vanished when the shot punched through and took off the back of his head, leaving behind mostly red mist and moist refuse.

Slown vomited, managing to turn to the side before he did. The little girl's mouth opened and shut, opened and shut while he retched on her.

Kane snatched the weapon from Slown's limp grip, and checked the bore. Empty. He tossed it to Walkowitz, who slung the weapon. To Slown, Kane said, "Welcome to manhood. When you're ready, we walk on."

For more, be sure to check out

Damnation Driven

The action packed second book in the

series, due out **August 2015!**

Also by Daniel R. Robichaud

Novels
From Hell's Heart

Collections
Derring-Do
Five Dark Enchantments
Five More Dark Enchantments
Ten Dark Enchantments

Individual Stories
The Samurai of Hell
Heed the Hell-Bound
Unforgiving and Cruel
Damnation's Steel

Ghostly Tales of the Balladeer
A Song to Soothe the Restless
Down to the Devil's House

Dark Fantasy Stories
Dust and Worms: A Weird Western

Heroic Fantasy Stories
A Matter for Amateurs
Curious Consumption
Killer's Honor
Vasily and the Beast Gods

Dark Enchantment Singles (Amazon.com Exclusives)
Ashes and Nails
Big Night for Daddy's Little Girl
Bootleg Images
Dust on Crust
Dzimba Dzemabwe
Hunter's Rite
Morning Glories
Of All the Things I've Lost . . .
Pear-Shaped
TBR

Also by Daniel (writing as C. C. Blake)

Novels
Darkest Dominions
The Devils of Los Angeles

Valkyrie Force Apocalyptic Thrillers
Wormtown Walkers
Damnation Driven
Amherst Annihilation

Short Novels
The Murder Cage

Collections
A Sense of Wonder
Bloody Business: Thrilling Tales of Undead Danger
Terrifying Tomorrows
Confess, Witch: Thrilling Tales of Occult Danger
Five Crimes
Five Micro Shocks
Five More Microshocks
In the Clutches of El Diablo: Sexy Suspense Adventures
Mystic Dangers: Thrilling Tales of Supernatural Adventure
Nightmare Stories
Publish and/or Perish: Unlikely Academic Adventures (forthcoming)
Nine Thrillers
Spicy Space Operas
Ten Micro Shocks

Individual Stories
Dark Fantasy Adventures
Countdown on Hex Island (with Kaysee Renee Robichaud)
Divinest Sense
I Own My Fears
The Sacrifice

Science Fiction Adventures
The Positronic Pretty: Rick Cave Space Opera Adventure
The Beauty Snatchers: Rick Cave Science Fiction Adventure
NAStar Driver (Vol. 1): Two Laps Around the Space Lanes
To Honor Her Father: A Science Fiction Revenge Story
Laurie Parker and the Intergalactic Girl Show
Fly By Night

Suspense Thrillers
The Ballad of the Cop's Gun
Chuck Cave and the Vanishing Vixen
Dark
Dirty
Fatal Femmes: Sexy Spy Adventures
G.I. Joe: Tight Spots
The Go-To Girl
Seller's Market
Trapped Like Rats
Wayne and Bean

Micro Shock Singles (Amazon.com Exclusives)
Best Spent Inside
Decisions Decisions
Finger to Allah
Kill Bell
Kill Die Coup
One Drop of Blood, One Year of Life
Spooky Yogurt
The Deciding Factor
What You Crave
What's In the Box?

About the Author

Daniel R. Robichaud lives and writes in Houston, Texas. Daniel holds degrees in Physics and English literature, and these two loves for science and story find their ways into his various occupations. He has been a medical researcher, an Igor for Hire, and a software architect developing controls and sensors for one of the most prestigious (and notorious) companies in the oil and gas industry. He has been a published writer for over fifteen years, responsible for hundreds of stories, poems and articles.

Under his own name, Daniel is an award nominated write of dark fantasy, poetry and plays. His most recent publications include the sword and sorcery short novel *From Hell's Heart* as well as the collections *Ten Dark Enchantments* and *Derring-Do*.

Under the C. C. Blake pseudonym, he is the author of numerous pulse pounding neo-pulp fiction and adventure stories. His serial character Chuck Cave started out in the award winning short story "Chuck Cave and the Vanishing Vixen," for Man's Story 2 magazine, and has since appeared in numerous stories and two novels, the crime fiction *The Devils of Los Angeles* and a sexy vampires novel, *Darkest Dominions*.

Valkyrie Force

The Valkyrie Force, a brand new military-themed zombie series, draws from his childhood love of G. I. Joe, *The Road Warrior*, 1980s action series novels like *The Executioner*, and George A. Romero movies.

www.ingramcontent.com/pod-product-compliance
Lightning Source LLC
Chambersburg PA
CBHW070550180626
46817CB00005B/1766